"Did you hear what I was saying?"

He stepped closer. He had to get her mind off this, and there was only one way he knew how.

He brought his lips down to hers, stopping her words.

The kiss was supposed to be a distraction. A way to stop her thinking about having heard him talking to an Omega agent. Light. Fun. Hint of sweet flirtation and possible promise of more.

But the moment their lips touched every agenda he had vanished. What he meant to be sweet and soft immediately turned heated.

What the hell was he doing?

He stepped back, giving him some much-needed distance and found her clear blue eyes blinking up at him as if she couldn't quite figure out what was going on.

I know the feeling, Peaches.

He gave her a smile and moved away, trying—way too late—to make this more casual. And fighting the fear that this was going to leave them both bloody in the end.

IN THE LAWMAN'S PROTECTION

USA TODAY Bestselling Author

JANIE CROUCH

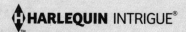

This book is dedicated to Harlequin. This is my twentieth book with this great publishing company, something I never thought would happen even in my wildest dreams. Thanks for taking a chance on me and being the driving force behind romance for readers all over the world.

Recycling programs for this product may not exist in your area.

ISBN-13: 978-1-335-63940-0

In the Lawman's Protection

Copyright © 2018 by Janie Crouch

All rights reserved. Except for use in any review, the reproduction or utilization of this work in whole or in part in any form by any electronic, mechanical or other means, now known or hereafter invented, including xerography, photocopying and recording, or in any information storage or retrieval system, is forbidden without the written permission of the publisher, Harlequin Enterprises Limited, 22 Adelaide St. West, 40th Floor, Toronto, Ontario M5H 4E3, Canada.

This is a work of fiction. Names, characters, places and incidents are either the product of the author's imagination or are used fictitiously, and any resemblance to actual persons, living or dead, business establishments, events or locales is entirely coincidental.

This edition published by arrangement with Harlequin Books S.A.

For questions and comments about the quality of this book, please contact us at CustomerService@Harlequin.com.

® and TM are trademarks of Harlequin Enterprises Limited or its corporate affiliates. Trademarks indicated with ® are registered in the United States Patent and Trademark Office, the Canadian Intellectual Property Office and in other countries.

Printed in U.S.A.

Janie Crouch has loved to read romance her whole life. This *USA TODAY* bestselling author cut her teeth on Harlequin Romance novels as a preteen, then moved on to a passion for romantic suspense as an adult. Janie lives with her husband and four children overseas. She enjoys traveling, long-distance running, movie watching, knitting and adventure/obstacle racing. You can find out more about her at janiecrouch.com.

Books by Janie Crouch

Harlequin Intrigue

Omega Sector: Under Siege

Daddy Defender
Protector's Instinct
Cease Fire
Major Crimes
Armed Response
In the Lawman's Protection

Omega Sector: Critical Response

Special Forces Savior
Fully Committed
Armored Attraction
Man of Action
Overwhelming Force
Battle Tested

Omega Sector

Infiltration
Countermeasures
Untraceable
Leverage

Primal Instinct

Visit the Author Profile page at Harlequin.com.

CAST OF CHARACTERS

Ren McClement—Omega Sector founding agent with highest levels of security clearance.

Natalie Anderson—Damien Freihof's ex-wife, who he believes is dead.

Damien Freihof—Terrorist mastermind determined to bring down Omega Sector piece by piece by doing what they did to him: destroying their loved ones.

Steve Drackett—Director of the Omega Sector Critical Response Division.

Brandon Han—Omega Sector Critical Response Division agent and profiler.

Andrea Gordon Han—Omega Sector behavioral analyst; married to Brandon.

Lillian Muir—Omega Sector Critical Response Division SWAT team member.

Philip Carnell—Undercover member of Omega Sector.

Roman Weber—Omega Sector Critical Response Division SWAT team member.

Ashton Fitzgerald—Sharpshooter for Omega Sector Critical Response Division's SWAT team.

Omega Sector—A multi-organizational law enforcement task force made up of the best agents our country has to offer.

Chapter One

For a dead woman, Natalie Anderson was pretty paranoid about security.

She rested her forehead against the back of the heavy wooden door. The closed, locked and completely bolted, heavy wooden door. And even though she hated herself for it, she reached down to double-check the security of the locks again.

Double-check, ha. Double-checking could be forgiven. This was more like octuple-check. And it wasn't just this door. It was every door in the house. And every window.

And she was about to start round nine. She had to stop herself. This could go on all night if she let it; she knew that for a fact.

"Get your sticky notes, kiddo," she muttered to herself. "Work the problem."

She'd discovered the sticky note trick around year two of being "dead." That if she put one of the sticky pieces of paper on each window and door after she was one hundred percent certain the locks were in place, she could finally stop checking it again. Didn't have to worry she'd accidentally missed one. Otherwise it was hours of the same thing over and over, just to be sure.

She grabbed the knockoff sticky papers she'd gotten from a discount store and began her process. She checked every single door—*again*—then every single window. The little yellow squares all over the place gave her a sense of security.

Although she had to fight the instinct to check them all one more time just to be absolutely sure.

She hadn't needed sticky notes in a while. Her tiny, threadbare apartment—not even a full studio, just a room and bathroom that was part of a garage—only had two windows and one door. That didn't take a whole lot of stationery to make her feel safe.

Agreeing to house-sit a gorgeous beach house in Santa Barbara had seemed liked such a great idea two weeks ago. Something different. Beautiful sunsets on the beach. A place where she could get out her paints, ones she'd caved and bought when she couldn't afford them, even though she hadn't painted in six years. Yeah, house-sitting had seemed like such a great idea.

Olivia, a waitress friend at the bar where Natalie worked in the evenings, had talked Natalie into it. Olivia was supposed to have been doing the house-sitting, but her mother had had a stroke and she'd had to go out of town.

So here Natalie was, in a million-dollar home with a view of the Pacific, and instead of cracking the doors to hear the sounds of the ocean or getting out her paints, she had every drape pulled tight and every door battened down enough to withstand a siege. Did she really wish she was smelling the motor oil that permeated everything in her apartment on the far east side of town rather than the brisk February California night air?

She turned away from the front door and forced herself to cross to the living room and sit on the couch. Once there the exhaustion nearly overwhelmed her, settling into her bones. Seven hours at her cleaning job today, then another six washing dishes at the bar.

That was her life almost every day. Seven days a week. For nearly the past six years.

None of the jobs paid even minimum wage. But they all paid in cash, and that was what mattered. She hadn't filled out any tax papers or had to show any ID. Because anyone who tried to pay Natalie Anderson Freihof would find out rather quickly that Mrs. Freihof died six years ago, caught in a freak shootout between law enforcement and some bank robbers.

The irony of that entire situation wasn't lost on her. Law enforcement had come for the robbers, never knowing there was a much bigger criminal—her husband—trapped right in the lobby with all the other victims. They could've made the world a much safer place by leaving the thugs with guns and masks and taking the man in the impeccable three-piece suit into custody. Would've saved a lot more lives.

Including Natalie's.

But she had made it away from Damien, thanks to some idiot bank robbers, gung-ho SWAT members and a freak biological hazard scare at the local hospital, which required the immediate cremation of all corpses that day.

In other words, chaos on multiple levels. But Natalie had taken the chance and run.

Whatever the reason it had all worked out, she wouldn't question. She was just glad it had. Just glad she had gotten away from the hell she'd been trapped in. If she had to work under the table, doing low-paying junk jobs for the rest of her life, she would do it. At least she was alive.

Most people would probably think staying completely under the radar even after all this time would be overkill, not that she had ever told anyone about her situation. That after a funeral and burial—even if it had been an empty casket—her husband would accept that she was dead. Wouldn't be searching for her.

But Natalie would put nothing past the methodical bastard that had systematically controlled her life and tortured her for years. Checking to make sure she wasn't drawing a paycheck years after she'd been declared dead? She could totally see Damien doing something like that. Then casually strolling through the door of her place of employment the next day.

She should probably move to Nebraska or Missouri where the cost of living wasn't so high or somewhere that wasn't SoCal so she wouldn't have to work so hard. Even the rent on her tiny apartment was ridiculous.

But California was the only place *he'd* ever said he hated. That he never wanted to step foot in again. Natalie had been praying that was true for six years and, so far, it had been. So she would stay here, even if she was tired. Even if fear was her constant companion. Even if half her salary was spent on sticky notes.

Agreeing to house-sit had been a mistake. The view was nice, as was the coffee machine she used to brew her cup in the mornings. And the linens were at least a three times higher thread count than she was used to. But the unfamiliarity of it all just added to her stress.

More windows to check. Longer bus rides to and from work.

The feeling like eyes were on her.

She'd fought that compulsion so often in the early days. The fear that she would get home and Damien would be there. Or that he was watching her from across the street. Ready to take her back into the hell he'd trapped her in for so long.

The feeling that she was being watched had to be just the unfamiliarity. The exhaustion. She needed sleep.

She wished she could convince herself that was the case.

It was so hard to know. In the early days, she'd so often given in to the panic. Let it dictate all her moves. She tried not to do that anymore, tried instead to make logical decisions based on actual circumstances rather than gut feelings.

Gut feelings couldn't be trusted. Her gut had told her that marrying Damien was a wise move, that he would provide her a happily-ever-after.

So she didn't trust her gut to tell her what to do now. Especially when she knew exhaustion was playing such a large factor in everything happening inside her head.

She hoped.

But she stood up and began checking the locks on all the windows and doors once more, despite the sticky notes. Trusting her gut or not, she knew sleep would not be coming. Not tonight. She couldn't shake the feeling.

Someone was watching out in the dark.

REN MCCLEMENT STRETCHED his long legs out in front of him in an attempt to get comfortable inside the Dodge Stratus. He was forty-one years old and one of the highest ranked members of Omega Sector, arguably one of the most prestigious law enforcement groups in the world. Hell, he'd *created* Omega Sector.

He should not be on a damned stakeout.

Any one of his colleagues would tell him the same thing: that there was other important work he could be doing. Although Ren didn't have an office at either the Critical Response Division HQ in Colorado or in Washington, DC, where the Covert Operations Division was located, at any given time he was a part of a dozen different operations, almost all of them clandestine. He'd advised two separate presidents on operational strategies in both foreign and domestic events.

And he'd been undercover for months at a time in some of the ugliest hellholes on earth—both geographically and situationally. He'd taken the ops nobody else wanted or could do. Stepped up to and over lines no one else was willing to cross in order to get the job done. Deep-cover operations where the line between who you were and the psychopath you pretended to be got pretty blurred.

He had to be able to live with that.

Ren McClement lived in darkness. Not only lived, *embraced* it. The dark was home for him. The dark was what allowed him to become whoever he needed to be in order to get the job done. To trick the worst of the worst into trusting him so he could make sure they could never harm anyone else again.

And if he sometimes forgot who he really was—the boy who grew up on a ranch in Montana with loving parents and a fierce need to be outdoors—he just considered that an occupational hazard.

If losing the real Ren meant that the world was a safer place, then so be it. He would sacrifice his past childhood so that future child-hoods would endure.

But normally stakeouts weren't part of his world-saving undertakings. Some grunt with much less experience and responsibility would be tasked to watch the very quiet beach house in Santa Barbara and could report back.

Not that there would be much to report.

This was night number five of watching Natalie Freihof inside this damn almost-mansion. Every night she came home late from the bar she'd been partying at, went inside and didn't come out until the dawn hours.

He had to admit, she was smart. Conscious of keeping a low profile. She kept her head down as she came in and out, always wearing nondescript jeans and a T-shirt, and caught a bus to get wherever she was going so it was much more difficult to follow her.

She went into one office building just after dawn on Mondays through Thursdays, and an entirely different one Fridays through Sundays. Both offices were in the process of being thoroughly investigated by Omega. He imagined at least one of the businesses in them was being used as a shell company of some kind. A front so Natalie could provide resources for her husband. It was just a matter of time before

Omega found out exactly what she was doing with which business.

Then some nights she would go to a bar a few miles away. Once more dressed in the jeans and shirt to go from place to place, which proved again how smart she was. If she needed to run, the clothing would allow her to blend in quickly and easily to almost any crowd. The comfortable athletic shoes would allow her to run.

He had no doubts she changed clothes once she was inside the bar for whatever it was she was doing. Meeting other clients or contacts? Or maybe just having a good time. She tended to stay until well after midnight on the nights she was there.

Evidently the dead Mrs. Freihof didn't require much sleep. Or partying, wining and dining were more important to her than rest. Either way, every time she left the bar, she was again changed into her nondescript clothes, her head was down and she was back on the bus.

The multi-million-dollar beach-front house was more along the lines of what Ren expected of Damien Freihof's wife. The deed wasn't in her name, of course, and the owners were also being investigated, although on the surface even Ren had to admit they looked clean.

The entire thing was smart. Savvy. Natalie had the weary bus commuter look down to a science. If Ren hadn't known it was all fake—that she lived in the lap of luxury while assisting a monster who had made it his mission in life to kill innocent people—he might have felt sorry for her. Something about the tall, willowy blonde brought out his protective instincts.

But Ren viciously tamped that down. What brought out his protective instincts more? The need to stop a killer before he struck again.

They didn't have a warrant to get inside the house, but that hadn't stopped Ren from going in while others were following Natalie to work. He'd been disappointed in what he'd found in the house.

Nothing.

But what had he been expecting? Natalie had successfully convinced the world she was dead for six years. Omega Sector had only discovered she was alive by sheer accident. Their photo-recognition software—part of it programmed to run 24/7 searching for any known associates of Damien Freihof—had tagged her in the background of a newspaper photo. She'd happened to be walking out of a building when a photographer snapped a picture of a group of teenagers receiving a science award.

Ren hardly expected to find anything now

that was going to provide irrefutable evidence that she was working with Freihof or providing him assistance. The only thing he'd seen that provided any evidence she'd been there at all had been the small indentation on the very edge of the king-size bed.

Natalie definitely wasn't rolling toward the middle of the bed, reaching for her husband. Of course, Damien would have to be called her ex-husband since he remarried after Natalie's "death."

That poor woman had died in a car accident just a year later. Dead wife number two. When Omega had found out that Natalie was in fact alive, they had exhumed two grave sites. One coffin had contained a body. Natalie's had not.

Legally, Natalie was no longer officially married to Freihof, due to his second marriage. Omega lawyers had already checked into that to make sure laws about testifying against one's spouse wouldn't come into play.

But married to him or not, if Natalie Freihof was helping Damien—which Ren had very little doubt she was—he would take her down.

Five days he'd been watching her, hoping she would slip up or get complacent and lead them to Freihof. The phones at the house were tapped, but she never used them. And if she had a cell phone, it was a burner that she didn't use at the house. No cell signals ever came from there.

So they were basically at a dead end. A place Ren didn't like to be and didn't find himself at very often.

It was time to shake things up. If they didn't put pressure on ex–Mrs. Freihof, she was never going to do anything reckless. It was time to force her hand.

Ren grabbed his phone and dialed a number. It wasn't even dawn here yet, and Colorado was only an hour ahead, but Steve Drackett still answered and sounded like he'd been awake for hours. Given that the man had a new baby it was entirely possible.

"Ren. Any change?" The head of the Omega Sector Critical Response Division skipped all formal greetings.

"Nothing. And no sign that she's going to do anything anytime soon. We need to prod her into action. Watching just isn't cutting it."

"I've had Brandon Han and Andrea Gordon-Han working on this. They're both pretty adamant that Natalie may be a victim, not an accomplice."

Ren glanced at the house again. Quiet. Almost deathly still. "Maybe." He doubted it. "But either way she's our best shot."

"There's something else you should know.

Six of the canisters in law enforcement offices around Atlanta have gone missing."

Ren's muttered curse under his breath was foul. Saul Poniard, the traitor inside Omega Sector who had been working with Freihof, had planted biological weapons in law enforcement offices throughout the country. He'd come within seconds of releasing them all and killing tens of thousands of law enforcement personnel two weeks ago.

"I thought we'd gotten all the canisters back into safe hands?"

"Finding them all has been more tricky than we anticipated. These were scheduled for pickup. And they were picked up and signed for, just not by the agents who were supposed to get them."

Ren cursed again. Six canisters of the biological contaminants was enough to take out half a city.

"The icing on the cake?" Steve continued. "Signed for by a D. Freihof. Bastard didn't even try to hide it, Ren. And we got an affirmative ID on him from a traffic cam in South Carolina. I've got some of my best agents there now."

Freihof with biological weapons was damn near the scariest thing Ren could imagine.

"We move tomorrow, Steve. We can't wait

any longer. I know it's a complicated operation, but it's our best bet."

"Roger that. You still want Brandon and Andrea to talk to her? Keep you out of the picture? If so, I'll send them out in a couple of hours. They can be at Natalie's doorstep by this afternoon."

"Yes." Ren could feel all the details of the plan floating around in his mind. "I'll watch from the surveillance truck. And I'll have everything ready. If this plays out the way I think it will, Natalie Freihof will be running into my arms soon enough."

Chapter Two

Natalie was getting home from work at two o'clock in the afternoon rather than two o'clock in the morning. Only seven hours of work rather than fourteen. She smiled wryly as she put the key into the lock of the beach house door. Practically a vacation.

And damn it, she was going to enjoy the beach. This house. Not let it make her feel panicked and trapped like last night. The sun was shining outside and she was going to revel in it. She'd fight the darkness tonight when it arrived.

She dropped the smaller backpack, the one she took with her everywhere, on the ground inside the bedroom door and opened the larger one resting next to it. She hadn't unpacked any of her clothes here at the beach house, but then again, she didn't have anything unpacked even when she stayed in her apartment. She'd trained herself to be ready to leave at a moment's notice.

And if she was tempted even for a second to let her guard down, to unpack and get comfortable, all she had to do was stretch her arms out over her head and feel the ache in her shoulder from where Damien had dislocated it not once but twice during their marriage.

Or go up on her tippy toes and feel that one ankle couldn't support her because of how it had broken when she'd fallen down the stairs, courtesy of her husband's shove.

Burn marks on the inside of her arm. Scars from restraints on her wrists and ankles.

And the fact that she still couldn't stand the snow.

Snow would haunt her until the day she died.

She ripped off her cleaning uniform of khaki pants and solid navy polo shirt, threw them over the back of the couch and put on a tank top and shorts. Damn it, Damien wasn't here. Couldn't hurt her. There was no snow. There was only California sunshine and a view of the beautiful Pacific Ocean. He would not steal this from her like he'd stolen so much. She would sit out on the deck and do nothing.

She was successful at that for all of ten minutes.

The knock on the door had her bolting from

her lazy sprawl in the hammock, her heart a hammer against her ribs. She looked at the front door, then at the stairs that led from the deck down to the street below. Should she run?

Her backpack was still inside. If she ran, she would have to leave everything behind. Money. Clothes. It wasn't much, but it was all she had.

The knock came again as she fought to decide what to do.

Damien wouldn't knock. She calmed a little as the words flowed through her. If Damien had found her he would not be knocking politely at the door.

This wasn't even her house. Chances were it was someone for the owners. Easy to get rid of. She walked inside to the front door, collecting herself.

As soon as she opened the door she knew she'd made a mistake.

Everything about the Asian man and smaller blonde woman, both dressed in carefully cut suits, screamed federal agents. Natalie should've chosen to take the stairs at the deck, to get out while she could. Leaving behind everything would've been better.

She forced herself to breathe at an even, normal pace. She eased the door more slightly closed, hoping if she needed to slam it and run she'd be able to.

"Can I help you?"

"Natalie?" The woman, four or five inches shorter than Natalie, with hair almost the same color blond, spoke.

"I'm sorry," Natalie said, avoiding the question. "This isn't my house. I'm just house-sitting for a friend."

Oh, crap, Natalie realized she didn't really know anything about the owners. She had their names written down somewhere on the instructions Olivia had given her, but didn't remember them offhand.

"But you're Natalie, right?" the woman asked again softly. The man moved slightly closer to the woman, almost as if he was going to step in front of her to protect her if she needed it. Like Natalie was going to jump out at her kicking and clawing. That was the last thing he needed to worry about.

She had to stay calm. "I think you have me confused with someone else. Like I said, this isn't my house, but I promise I'm not here illegally." She inched the door farther closed.

The woman just reached down into her bag and pulled out a photograph, sticking it directly in front of Natalie's face.

Fear closed around her throat. It was a shot

of her and Damien on their wedding day, smiling at one another. Natalie's hair had been much longer, her cheeks fuller, her smile genuine.

She felt the room begin to spin.

"Whoa, are you okay?" It was the man this time. He pushed the door open and grabbed Natalie's arm before she could fall. "Just take a breath, all right? We just want to ask some questions."

Natalie's knees couldn't hold her anymore and the guy helped lower her to a sitting position on the floor leaning back against the wall next to the door. Both he and the woman took advantage of Natalie's moment of weakness to enter the house, closing the door behind them.

"You shouldn't be here," Natalie said again. "This isn't my house."

The two people looked at each other, the man giving the woman a slight nod. Some sort of secret agent code, for sure. Then they both looked back at her, squatting down so they were closer to her, eye to eye.

"I'm Andrea," the woman said. "And this is my husband, Brandon."

No last names. No credentials. Natalie didn't want to push, but at least they weren't reading her her Miranda rights.

Of course, the afternoon was still young.

"I'm sorry, I'm not feeling well," Natalie finally responded. "I appreciate your help, but I'm going to have to ask you to leave. Like I said, this isn't my house and I had express instructions that I wasn't to have anyone else here while the owners are away."

"Just let us help you get over to the couch," the man, *Brandon*, said. "Just to make sure you're okay."

If that would get them to leave, then great. "Fine."

She took the hands both of them outstretched and rose. They walked her over to the couch, and she sat back down, feeling the shirt and pants she'd thrown over it rub against her back.

"Thanks. If you guys don't mind seeing yourselves out, that would be great." Natalie would be seeing herself out as soon as they were gone.

Out of the entire state.

"It's obvious you don't want to talk to us," Andrea said, taking a seat in the chair across from Natalie, much to her dismay. "We'd just like you to listen for a few minutes."

What could she do? Natalie nodded slowly.

"We're trying to find Damien Freihof," Brandon said, coming to stand next to his wife, still staying within a protective reach.

Natalie fought not to blanch, not to give anything away, when it was all she could do not to bolt. "I'm sorry. I think you have mistaken me for someone else."

It was just as flimsy the third time, but it was all she had—hanging on to the possibility that they weren't exactly sure who she was. Although the wedding picture was pretty damning.

But at least if they were looking for Damien, they hadn't been sent by him.

"Falsifying a death report is illegal," Brandon continued, but then stopped with just the slightest touch on his arm by Andrea.

Just a single touch. What would it be like to have someone respect you and care for you so much that the touch of fingertips communicated something both ways? Something Brandon obviously respected.

Natalie had never had that in her entire life.

"It's imperative that we find Damien Freihof," Andrea said. "Lives are at stake."

Natalie just stared. She couldn't help them even if she wanted to. She'd known better than to keep tabs on Damien—the man was near genius with a computer. He would've found out.

She shrugged. "I can't help you."

"Maybe we can help *you*," Andrea continued. "Keep you safe, if that's part of your concerns."

Natalie just shrugged again.

"We're talking about more than just Brandon and me, of course," Andrea continued. "An entire team. A very strong group of people who would help you."

For just a second Natalie wanted to cave, to find out more, to trust someone so she wouldn't have to live in fear all the time. But she squashed it down. She couldn't trust anyone. All she could do was run.

Because the truth was, if these people had found her, Damien could, too. She needed to get them out of here.

"Look, I'm sorry. I know I look a lot like that woman in the picture. Quite the doppelgänger." She gave a laugh that sounded fake even to her own ears. "But that's not me. I can see how you would think that it is, but it's just not. I've never been married."

She stood up and walked toward the massive kitchen that was open to the living room, gripping the island to try to steady herself. "I don't want to be rude, but I've got appointments and stuff scheduled for this afternoon. So I'm going to have to ask you to leave."

What was she going to do if they didn't

leave? Threaten to call the police? Natalie wasn't capable of that kind of bluff.

"Falsifying your own death is illegal," Brandon said again. Natalie just stared at him unflinchingly.

Her choice had been between faking her own death or eventually ending up actually dead. She had no doubt the course she'd been on with Damien would've led to her eventual death.

So no matter how crappy her life was now, how many jobs she had to work to survive, how many sticky notes she had to put on windows to convince herself she was safe and how accusingly this law enforcement agent looked at her now…she'd definitely made the right choice.

"I'm sure it is, Officer…"

The two looked at each other again, secret agent code with some husband/wife telepathy thrown in. They got up and walked closer to her in the kitchen, where she was filling a cup with water from the tap.

"My name is Brandon Han," he finally said. "I'm an agent with Omega Sector's Critical Response Division."

They were both staring at her as if this would cause some big reaction. Natalie had no idea what they were talking about. She'd never heard of Omega Sector and wasn't about to ask any questions.

They were cops. They could bring to light the fact that she was still alive, if they hadn't already. And maybe she might do a year or two in prison for faking her death, but that would be nothing compared to what she would face after she got out.

"Okay, Agent Han. I'm still not who you think I am. I'm sorry I can't help you. But I'm still going to need to ask you to leave."

"Omega Sector can protect you," Agent Han continued as if she hadn't spoken. "We can make sure the slate is wiped clean. No jail time for you for falsifying. If there is something else, we can maybe make a deal for that, too."

Something else? What the hell else illegal did they think she'd done? Maybe they were talking about taxes or something. That could add up to more jail time.

Which would *still* be safer than being out on the streets if Damien knew she was alive. God, she had to get out of here. The panic was crawling all over her body, slimy and slick. She couldn't get rid of it. Just needed to get out of here. Right. Now.

"Please go." She forced the hoarse words past her throat and nearly buckled in relief when they turned toward the door without further argument. Brandon reached into his pocket and grabbed a card. Natalie took it, although she never planned to even so much as glance at it again.

"Call us if anything changes," Brandon said as Natalie opened the door and allowed them to walk through. "Anything. At any time. And especially if you happen to see Damien Freihof. And remember, the earlier you get us information, the better it will go for you. Deals for keeping you out of prison are only good when they help both sides."

"I'm still not your person. Sorry." She smiled in as friendly a manner as she could manage.

She was closing the door behind them when at the very last second Andrea stopped her with a hand on the door. It was only open a crack and Natalie had stepped behind it so she couldn't see them. She considered just shutting it until she heard Andrea's words.

"Damien Freihof got remarried to someone else two years after his wife Natalie died. Because no body for Natalie was ever identified, he was required to file for divorce before he could remarry. So no matter what, according to state laws, his marriage with Natalie is null and void even if she magically reappeared alive somewhere."

Marriage was null and void. Natalie gripped the door, barely able to contain a sob.

"Call us, Natalie. We want to help." Andrea took the pressure off the door and it slid shut, leaving Natalie alone. She turned and slid her back all the way down the wood until she reached the ground, tears streaming out of her eyes.

She wasn't married to Damien anymore. No matter what, she wasn't married to him.

Until this moment she'd had no idea that had even been a concern, but now she realized it had been a huge one. That if she was discovered alive she'd be returned to her *husband.* The man who had abused her for years.

But that would never happen because they weren't married anymore. She took a shuddery breath, pulling that fact deep into her soul. Damien would never be her husband again.

That didn't mean he wouldn't kill her if he found her.

She got up off the ground. She had to get going right now.

Because lack of an official piece of paper calling them married was not going to stop Damien from hunting her if he found out she was alive. California was no longer safe.

She needed to run.

Chapter Three

"Did you get what you needed?" Brandon asked as he and Andrea stepped into the surveillance van that was parked farther down the block from the beach house.

Ren shrugged. "I didn't get a location on Freihof, so not exactly."

He'd had both audio and partial video of Andrea and Brandon's discussion with Natalie. The questioning had gone down like he'd expected it would: without any cooperation from her.

"Maybe we should've pushed harder," Brandon said, sitting in the van's only other seat and pulling his wife onto his lap.

"No." Ren shook his head, glancing at the feed they had of the front of the house. "We needed to keep the situation open. Make Natalie think that she has options, can still get word to Freihof if she wants to. Maybe run to him and both of them flee the country."

Whatever she did, they would be watching.

"I don't think she's working with him," Andrea said. "I should've brought up the not-married aspect earlier. That was key, I realize now. If I had been able to see her when I said that, I'd be able to tell a lot more about her."

Andrea was a gifted behavioral analyst. Her abilities to read people's nonverbal cues were uncanny.

"Do you think she was upset that she's not legally married to him anymore?"

She gave a small shrug. "I don't know for sure, since I wasn't able to see her. But the news definitely affected her. Her knuckles were white in her grip and she stopped pushing on the door because she wanted to hear what I had to say."

"She could've been upset because Freihof hadn't told her about the divorce. Any wife would be pretty miffed to get that news."

Andrea nodded. "That's possible, certainly."

Ren studied her. "But you don't think so."

Brandon curled his arm around his wife in support. Out of everyone in Omega Sector, these two had had the most contact with Damien Freihof. Freihof had written letters to Andrea while in prison, then had come after her once he'd escaped.

"Freihof is obsessive. Controlling," Brandon

said. "Hell, the man once saved Andrea's life just because he wanted to kill her himself."

Andrea nodded, leaning into Brandon. "Freihof is a master puppeteer. He's been collecting people who have some sort of gripe with Omega for months. Inciting them to violence. Getting them to do his dirty work for him. Or at least trying to."

The number of people connected to Omega who had been hurt or killed by either Freihof or one of his *puppets* over the last few months had been pretty staggering. Omega was still reeling. It was the reason Ren was on this case personally.

"Agreed." Ren nodded. "But what does this mean with Natalie? She didn't even admit to being Natalie Freihof much less give any info on him."

"There's something we're missing," Andrea said. "Honestly, I'm not sure exactly what it is, but I know it's important. We don't have all the information."

Ren didn't need all the information to make his move. "It doesn't matter. Your presence shook her up. She'll do something now. Hopefully lead us directly to her not-husband husband."

Andrea tilted her head to the side. Ren could feel her studying him. Gauging his nonverbal behavior. "And if she doesn't know where he is? If she's been *dead* all this time to get away from him?"

"She's been running three businesses without anyone even knowing she's alive. She's either one hell of a businesswoman or she's doing it for Freihof."

Andrea shrugged again. "All I'm saying is that we're missing pieces of information. Important pieces."

"That's why I'm going to be ready for anything. She's going to run. Hopefully trying to get somewhere where she thinks it's safe to contact Freihof. Where she's *forced* to contact Freihof. We're just going to make sure we control that spot when she does."

"And if she really doesn't know where he is? If she's been trying to stay away from him all this time? Hide from him?"

Highly unlikely, but Ren was willing to consider it. "Then we go to plan B. If she can't take us to Freihof, then we use Freihof's obsession to get him to come to her."

"That may be risking her life," Andrea said quietly.

"Natalie is a criminal here. Let's not forget that. She could've gone to law enforcement if she wanted to get away from her husband. It's much more likely that the two of them have been in on this together the whole time. That Freihof is trusting her to run her businesses to get him money."

"She didn't recognize Omega Sector at all when we mentioned who we were with," Brandon said. "Even I could tell that, and I'm not nearly as gifted at reading people. If she's working with Freihof, he's keeping huge chunks of information from her."

Or maybe she was just a much better liar than they were giving her credit for. Trained by Freihof to completely school her nonverbal reactions so they couldn't read her. "Look, I don't have all the answers. All I know is we're out of time, especially now that Freihof has those canisters. We shook things up, caught Natalie unaware. That's good. Now I suspect that tonight or early tomorrow she's going to make a break for it. We watch carefully and—"

Ren's words were cut off by Brandon's muttered curse. He pointed at the screen. "Actually, looks like she's already on the run."

The screen showed Natalie, the small backpack she always carried over one shoulder and a larger one over the other, already on the move, coming out her front door.

"Damn it, I wasn't expecting her to move

that fast. Get Lillian Muir on the phone and tell her to get in place down at the bus station."

Andrea stood and grabbed her phone.

"There weren't any calls from the house phone or the taps would've automatically turned on," Ren said. "She must have already had an emergency plan in place. Which doesn't strengthen the case for her being an innocent party."

"Unless she's just that scared," Brandon reasoned.

"Lillian will be at the downtown bus station in fifteen minutes," Andrea said, disconnecting the call. "It might be cutting it a little close if Natalie goes straight there, but Lillian should make it."

"Good. Muir is a good choice. If you don't know her, her size helps her come across as very nonthreatening. Natalie will respond to the suggestion more easily."

They needed to direct Natalie's path without making her suspicious.

"Brandon and I want to stop Freihof more than anyone," Andrea said, staring at him. "Trust me, I can still feel the explosives he strapped around my neck. So I hope you can get what you need from Natalie, Ren. And in a lot of ways I hope you're right and she is working with Freihof."

"You do?"

"Yes. Because if not, we're about to ruin an innocent woman's life."

NATALIE HAD BEEN taking the bus from the Santa Barbara oceanfront to downtown since she started house-sitting two weeks ago. She'd always been cautiously aware of anyone around her.

Now she was downright suspicious.

Were some of these people cops? Were they following her? Did they work for that Omega-whatever that Brandon and Andrea mentioned?

Nobody seemed to be paying any attention to her, which she hoped was a good sign. Maybe she had gotten out faster than the cops had expected. She'd grabbed her bug-out bag and left.

That was the point of a bug-out bag, right? So you could bug-out the instant you needed to.

Her bag wasn't a true survivalist kit, but it had changes of clothes, all her spare cash, some nutrition bars and a bottle-size water filtration system. It even contained a high-end sleeping bag that folded into the size of a bowling ball, but only weighed a pound and a half.

She'd balked at the price at the time, but now took comfort in knowing that if she needed to walk or hitchhike out of California, she could. Although her paints would have to go if she did that, which she hated to even consider, hoping to one day get the courage to use them again.

But there was no way she was staying here, even though she was losing her only means of employment. There had to be somewhere she could go where law enforcement wouldn't find her. She wasn't a violent criminal. Her picture wasn't going to show up on some Most Wanted list at the post office.

But she wanted to get as far away from here as possible. She would start heading to the East Coast—Boston or New York or Atlanta—somewhere where she could get lost in the crowd.

Flying was out since that required an ID, but she was hoping to get a jump on her escape by catching the first bus out. Hopefully it would take a day or two before the agents came back—and Natalie had no doubts they'd be back—and discovered she was gone.

Fifteen minutes after she left the beach house she was stepping off the bus in downtown Santa Barbara. The bus station, pretty tiny and nondescript, was another quarter mile down the main drag, far enough away from the tourist section to not be an eyesore.

The station was really just a large room with a series of benches and hard plastic chairs, and a small office where the ticket seller sat behind a glassed-in counter. The room was empty and the man working behind the counter was reading a magazine.

The first thing she needed to decide was where she wanted to go. But honestly, she didn't care. She would just see what was available.

"Can I help you?" the guy asked without looking up from his magazine as Natalie stepped up to the counter.

The door opened behind him. "Hey, George. Need you out here."

George turned from Natalie. "What? Who are—"

"The main office is on the line and some bigwig asked for you by name." The dark-haired woman in her midthirties, wearing the same uniform as George, walked into the small office and squeezed his shoulders, obviously urging him to stand. "Dude, just go. Rick's got the call on hold in his office. He sent me in here to relieve you."

George just looked confused. "But who are—"

The woman glanced over at Natalie and

rolled her eyes with a look that screamed, *Men. Am I right?* "George, honey, I don't know who it is. But I'm thinking promotion, so just go."

George stood. "Yeah, okay. A promotion would be good. Um, you're okay here?"

The woman rolled her eyes again before shooing him out. "No need to mansplain it. Lily's got it handled." Once George was out the back door, Lily turned back around to Natalie. "Okay! What can I do for you now that we've got the dead weight out of the room?" She winked at Natalie again.

Despite the panic crushing down on her, Natalie had to smile at the pocket-size woman who'd handled George so deftly.

"I need a ticket."

"That I can do. Where're you headed and when do you want to go there? We've got some great sales coming up next week if you want to go north."

"No, next week won't work. I know it will cost me more, but I need to go today."

Lily smiled. "No problem. Where to?"

"What are my options?"

"We have daily buses that go to Los Angeles, San Francisco and Las Vegas. From any of those you can get to just about anywhere. Where are you ultimately trying to get to?"

Natalie shifted back and forth, finding it difficult to look the friendly woman in the eye. "East Coast. Honestly, anywhere. But I was thinking Atlanta or maybe Philadelphia. I just need to get out of here today."

"I see. Well, do you prefer Atlanta over Philadelphia?"

Atlanta would be less cold and didn't tend to get snow. "Sure. Atlanta. But just…it's important that I leave as soon as possible."

Lily nodded, a little more solemn. "Okay, hon. Let me see what I can find."

Natalie waited as Lily began typing. After a few moments, a frown marred her forehead and a minute after that she began to grumble.

"Is there a problem?" Natalie finally asked.

"There's a California drivers' strike affecting buses from both LA and San Francisco. So neither of those are available for the next few days."

"Okay. What about Vegas?"

Lily nodded. "I'm checking that now."

The woman's fingers flew along the keyboard. Her grimace didn't reassure Natalie. "Completely full until Saturday. I'm so sorry, honey. What about flights? I know our municipal airport isn't much, but they have some flights. Or renting a car?"

Natalie could feel the panic clawing up inside her again. Neither of those would work;

both required identification that would put her in the system, making note of where she started and where she ended.

To her utter dismay she could feel tears welling up in her eyes. God, she could not lose it in the middle of this tiny busy station. She just needed to get out. She would hitchhike or walk.

"No, that won't work. Thanks for your help," she muttered, trying to wipe her eyes before the tears fell.

She was almost to the door when Lily called out. "Hang on there a second, hon, do you have any problems with trains?"

Natalie stopped and turned slowly. "Trains?"

Lily motioned for her to come back to the window and she did. "Look, you can't mention this to anyone here, and we need to handle it before George gets back from his big promotion or whatever."

"The bus station sells train tickets?"

She shook her head. "No, but we have access to information and ticketing about flights and trains in case of emergencies. Normally I wouldn't even mention it, but since you need to leave today and can't get out on a bus…"

"I didn't even know there were trains around here."

"Yeah, this one is a little weird. It's actually a freight train, but it has one passenger car. Sells up to twelve seats that can recline for sleeping. It's no frills…you have to bring food or grab some at the scheduled stops. One shared bathroom. But it's not too bad. My cousin took it a couple months ago—she's afraid of flying—and enjoyed it. Goes from here to Saint Louis. Takes four days."

A train. Natalie had never even thought of that possibility.

"What would I need to get a ticket?"

"Just cash or a credit card, just like a bus ticket." Lily quoted the price, which wasn't much more than a bus. "It only runs on Wednesdays, so you're pretty lucky. But if you're really trying to get out of here today, it sounds like it's your best bet. As long as you don't mind not having many people to talk to."

"Actually, that sounds kind of perfect. I just need some time to myself."

Lily grinned. "Every woman does at one time or another, sweetie."

Within five minutes Lily had printed her a ticket and given her directions to the train station. Natalie had to walk quickly to grab a sandwich and snacks at the grocery store and make it to the south side of town in time for departure. She was pretty nervous when she arrived at the train yard, hoping she hadn't made a huge mistake. But an employee pointed her in the right direction and a few minutes later she was climbing into the passenger car with just five minutes to spare.

She could barely believe her luck. It was perfect. Wide seats in groups of four—two each facing each other—with a table in the middle. They would be much more comfortable than the cramped constraints of a bus. Plus large windows where she'd be able to see as they crossed the country. There were three groups of seats, and Natalie's ticket was for one of the empty groups. Even better. Maybe no one else would get on.

There were only three other passengers. Across the aisle was an older woman reading a book and a younger man in a hoodie with headphones on sitting across from her. Natalie shifted so she could see the seats behind her.

Her breath caught in her throat at the man sitting in the seat. He looked up from the papers and computer on the table in front of him to glance out the window as a whistle blew, giving Natalie a view of his carved jaw and strong chin. His brown hair was thick and full, a little messy like he'd been running his fingers through it.

She knew she was staring but couldn't quite help herself. There was a ruggedness about his face that drew her. He looked away from the window, catching her ogling, his green eyes pinning hers. Before she could look away with embarrassment, he nodded slightly, then resumed the reading of his papers.

At that moment the train gave a little jerk as it started forward. Natalie took her seat and watched out the window as she left Santa Barbara behind.

No one knew she was here. No one knew where she was going.

Then why did she feel like she was in more danger than ever?

Chapter Four

Lillian Muir deserved an Oscar. Ren had watched as the woman quite deftly handled George even though Natalie had beat her to the bus station by a couple of minutes. If Lillian hadn't been able to get George out of the office she would've never been able to lie to Natalie about all the buses and get her on this train.

Score one for Omega Sector. And given how Lillian Muir didn't usually do undercover—she was a kick-ass SWAT team member who could kill any given person a dozen different ways with her tiny bare hands—she truly had been amazing. The perfect blend of friendly and business that had sold Natalie on this venture.

A venture that wouldn't have even been an option without the funding of Joe Matarazzo, another member of Omega Sector who also happened to be a multimillionaire. Joe wanted Freihof caught and behind bars so he and his pregnant wife could live in peace without worrying that they were next in line for a madman to attack. Funding this little field trip had been a no-brainer for Joe.

They'd been on the train nearly thirty-six hours. Natalie had kept to herself all of that time, mostly just staring out the window. The other two people in the car were both Omega personnel. The older woman, Madeline, was a retired agent who now worked as an analyst. The younger guy was Philip Carnell, not Ren's first choice, but he was someone who wanted Freihof off the streets pretty badly after getting stabbed a few weeks ago by one of the villain's cronies.

Natalie hadn't spoken to either of them. And, after looking at Ren that one time as the train left Santa Barbara, hadn't interacted with him, either. Not that he'd expected her to be the life of the party.

The train had stopped once at its scheduled point, east of Las Vegas. Everyone had gotten out and bought food and any supplies they needed. Agents had been following Natalie discreetly in case she bolted, but she'd actually been the first one back on the train.

They hadn't gotten very far before Philip, still dressed in a hoodie, swung casually across the aisle and sat right next to Natalie.

Ren leaned a little toward them so he could see what was happening more clearly. She had already stiffened and was leaning away from Philip, not looking at him at all.

Exactly what they had been hoping for when they'd come up with the plan of Philip turning on the obnoxious.

"Hey, you want some of my sandwich?" He was barely understandable over his chewing.

"No, thank you." Natalie didn't look away from the window. "I bought food at the stop."

Philip just leaned in closer and waved the sub sandwich in front of her face. "Are you sure? It's really good."

"No, I just want to be left alone."

"Aw, c'mon," Philip whined, slurring his words a little as though he'd been drinking. "It's getting dark. There's nothing to look at out the window. Why don't you talk to me instead? I'm tired of sitting by that old lady. Tell me a little about yourself."

Ren could see Natalie growing stiffer with every word. She didn't respond to Philip, just kept staring out the window.

"All I want to do is chat," he continued. "We've got a long way to Saint Louis. Just talk to me."

She finally glanced at him before immediately moving her gaze back to the window.

"I'm not interested in talking. I just want to be left alone."

"Really?" Philip sneered. "You think you're too good to talk to me, is that it? Well, that's okay, I can just stay here and get close to you. How about that?"

Natalie's spine was ramrod straight as Philip drew closer. She was all but pressed up against the window, but Ren caught a glimpse of one little fist tightening into a ball. He wondered what she would do if he wasn't about to intervene for the sake of the mission. He almost wanted to find out.

"Just leave me alone."

"I'm not talking about anything crazy, baby, unless you're interested in a little alone time in the bathroom or something like that." Philip leaned even closer.

That was Ren's cue.

He stood and crossed over to their seats. "Look, I think the lady has made it pretty clear that she doesn't want to talk to you."

Natalie peeked up at him, concern flashing in her blue eyes. Philip just kept staring at her. "Step back, man. This has nothing to do with you."

"Considering how small this train car is and that you're a little drunk and pretty loud, I think it does have to do with me."

Philip snickered. "Fine. We'll be quiet. Won't we, sweetheart?"

He reached toward Natalie and she flinched. Ren found it took much less acting than he'd thought to reach over and grab Philip's wrist and yank it backward away from her.

"Dude!"

Without effort, Ren bent Philip's arm into a position that wouldn't take more than a flick of his wrist to break it. "I'm pretty sure the lady doesn't want you to touch her." Color had leached from her face. "Is that right, ma'am?"

She nodded.

Ren released Philip's arm, and slapped him on the shoulder almost good-naturedly. "Why don't we just get one of the train officials to come back here and sort out the seating arrangement?"

If possible, Natalie's face lost even more color. "No, that's not necessary. I'm just not interested in talking to anyone."

Ren looked at Philip. "Why don't you just go on back to your assigned seat? Like she said, she's not here for conversation."

"I don't think it's fair that you both get your own sets of seats and I have to share with the old lady," Philip whined.

Ren glanced over at Natalie, who was still looking like she wanted to find some way to jump off the moving train, then back to Philip, who was doing a pretty damned good job of staying on script.

"Why don't you take my seat for a while? That way you'll have your own set and can spread out and get comfortable." His eyes flickered to Natalie. "I'll sit here if that's okay since I have work to do and am not looking for any conversation. Would that be okay?"

She looked back and forth between him and Philip. She didn't like it, he could tell. But when her eyes rested on Philip it was in distaste. When they rested on him it was in...*fear*.

Either he was projecting his intent in some way he wasn't aware of, or Natalie was very astute. Regardless, he was going to need to handle her with the utmost care if he was going to get her to trust him.

"Um..." She bit on her lip.

Ren gave her a friendly smile. "I understand. Just hang on a second and let me make a call up to the conductor." There was a phone near the front of the car that allowed passengers to make calls to the train officials if needed. Train officials that were all, for the most part, Omega Sector agents for this journey. "We can get this sorted out so you don't have to worry."

"No," she said quickly. "No, it's fine. If you

don't mind giving up your seat, it would be fine with me if you sit here."

Ren raised an eyebrow at Philip. "Okay with you?"

Philip looked over at Natalie and shrugged. "Your loss." Then got up and sauntered over to Ren's seats.

Philip winked at Ren as he followed him and grabbed his stuff. Ren gave the younger man a little nod. So far, everything was going as planned. Hopefully Ren's gesture of help would soften Natalie slightly toward him.

A few moments later he had his papers and laptop in hand and moved to the set of seats facing Natalie. He chose the seat near the aisle so both of them could stretch their legs without hitting each other.

She gave him a soft smile. Looking at her like this for the first time—not a photograph of her or through a recording device—Ren was almost struck dumb by her beauty. Straight blond hair that was in a braid that fell over her shoulder, wide crystal-blue eyes.

Lips so full and pouty they made him forget for a moment that she was most likely working with a man who had killed multiple innocent people and planned to continue.

No matter how angelic she looked—whatever air of innocence and fragility she gave off—Ren could not forget she was the enemy.

He smiled at her. "I promise, no talking."

She gave a little laugh. "You don't have a sandwich you're going to wave in my face, do you?"

"No, left all my sandwich weapons at home."

"Ah, hope we're not ambushed, then, or else you won't be much help." She gestured toward his computer. "I'll let you get back to work. Thanks again for the rescue."

She turned back to the window but Ren could see her checking him out in the reflection. And once it got dark she didn't have the excuse to stare out it anymore. She just sat there for a long time, looking at her hands folded in her lap.

"Do you not get cell coverage on your phone out here?" he finally asked. He could understand if she didn't want to contact Freihof, but surely there was something more interesting to do than just stare at her hands.

Her eyes flew to his. "I'm sorry?"

"People are on their phones all the time. It's unusual to see someone without one these days. I thought maybe yours just doesn't have coverage."

She shifted a little in her seat. "Oh, yeah. That's it. No coverage."

"No games or anything? E-reader?"

She shifted again, looking away. "My phone…isn't working right. So, not having coverage doesn't matter. And it's not much use for anything else."

He gave her his friendliest smile. "Going to be a long trip without anything to do. Or maybe you just prefer paper books?"

That got him a real smile. "Actually, I love paper books. But I didn't have a chance to buy any before I left."

"Sudden trip or are you like me, a last-minute packer?"

She relaxed just the slightest bit. "A little of both, I guess. Wasn't planning on taking the train, but the bus was full."

Ren nodded. "Yeah, the strike. What a mess." He shut his computer, watching to see if she would tense and turn away, pleased when she didn't. "I suppose you're going to mock me now."

Those blue eyes flew to his. "I am? Why?"

"Because of my fear of flying. I just can't stand the thought of being in an airplane. Therefore, my life involves a lot of buses, driving or, in this case, trains."

"What do you do?"

"I have a sheep and dairy farm in Montana." Damn it, where the hell had that come from?

A small auto parts store owner in Saint Louis. That was supposed to be his cover, something nondescript and not very memorable.

Why the hell had he told her the truth? He did have a sheep and dairy farm in Montana. His parents and brother lived and worked there. Ren had been itching to get back there himself.

But he definitely had not been planning to tell his suspect about it.

"Oh, wow, like cows and sheep?" She sounded a little excited before laughing harshly at herself. "Of course cows and sheep. I'm an idiot."

"Nah, don't say that. But yes, cows and sheep. We sell wool to some boutique stores out in California and across the country."

Damn it, more truth. But he was committed to it now, so he'd have to stick with it.

"That's pretty interesting. I've always loved animals, but…"

Only when it became obvious she wasn't going to finish did he prompt her. "But what?" he asked gently.

She looked back out to the blackened window for the longest time. "But having a pet or being around them just never worked out for me."

"Did you know that during WWI President Woodrow Wilson had a flock of sheep trim the White House lawn?"

She laughed, then looked surprised by the sound. "You're making that up."

"I'm not, Scout's honor." She liked animals? That he could give her. "My family got into sheep and dairy farming because my mother loved animals and couldn't stand the thought of slaughter. So sheep and dairy cows it became."

He told her some more entertaining stories about growing up with his brother on the farm, about getting chased around by chickens when he was a toddler and how his brother, Will, had thought that black sheep were dirty and tried to wash one when he was young.

And damned if he hadn't used Will's real name. A pretty common name, but still.

By the time he'd finished she almost looked like a completely different person. Her face was more relaxed, unguarded. Her long legs were tucked up under her as she'd turned to the side to listen to him, head against her seat, playing with the braid over one shoulder.

Every time he'd stopped telling a story, tried to get the conversation turned back to her, she'd asked another question about his life. Some downright insightful.

Had his father considered becoming a large-animal vet at one time? Yes, until he'd realized he wanted to own his animals and farm.

Did his mother ever knit them anything

from a particular sheep they'd loved? Yes. Ren still had a sweater she'd made him from a sheep he'd once carried home after it had broken its leg.

Had he and his brother both reached a point where they'd felt trapped by the farm and wanted to get away?

That one wasn't as easy to answer. Yes, Ren had left just after high school, deciding he'd preferred the excitement of joining the army than staying there any longer. The army had fast realized his ability to pick up new skills quickly, as well as his natural strength and intelligence. They'd fast-tracked him into special forces.

Ren had loved the army but had gotten out after six years when he was approached to start a special law enforcement task group that would be made up of the best agents and ex-soldiers the country had to offer. He'd birthed Omega Sector. And had been fighting bad guys ever since.

Like the bad guy sitting across from him now, with alabaster skin, her blue eyes drooping. She would've fooled him, he had to admit. If he hadn't already known what she was capable of, he wouldn't have believed it.

So yeah, he'd left the farm because it had made him feel trapped. Like nothing ever happened there. But he was beginning to realize how wrong that was. Maybe shootouts and arrests didn't happen there, but life did.

Light did.

He'd been living in the darkness so long that light was starting to seem damn more appealing.

"You going to go to sleep there, Peaches?"

One eyebrow cocked. "Peaches?"

He shrugged. "Your skin. Just looks smooth, like peaches and cream. My mom used to make it for us." Damn it, the truth. Again.

"Yeah, I'm a little tired. My name's Natalie, by the way."

He smiled. "I'm Warren Thompson, but generally go by Ren. Get some rest. I'll make sure no one attacks you with a sandwich. We've got a long way to go."

Plus, it would make it much easier for him to do what he was about to do if she was already out.

Her nod was full of trust, and just for a second guilt ate at Ren. It didn't get any better when she tucked herself into a tighter ball on her seat a few minutes later, one small hand curled under her chin.

He forced the feelings away. He wasn't dragging her into the darkness; she already lived there.

He just hoped he'd be able to find his way back to the light when this was all over. After what he had to do. Because the light had never seemed so far away.

Chapter Five

Natalie dreamed of sheep. All kinds. Baby lambs, adults heavy with wool and some that had just been shaved. She dreamed of sweaters and yarn and of a special sheep that had to be carried back to the safety of the farm.

She sat and watched as the man she'd listened to for hours, would've listened to for the rest of her life if she could've, ran around her with the sheep. Would ask her to count them, to make sure they didn't get lost in the darkness.

It was a crazy dream, because she knew she was dreaming, knew this wasn't real. She felt funny, like she was moving.

She was on a train, her tired brain remembered, but her eyes refused to open. But the movement felt different. Like she was being carried somewhere.

But she didn't want to go anywhere else;

she just wanted to stay here on the nice farm with the sheep.

"No, please," she murmured.

"Shh," someone said. "You're just dreaming."

That voice, that smoky, sexy voice again. She didn't want it to stop. Ren's voice.

"Sheep," she said, hoping he'd understand. She wanted him to tell her more stories.

"Yes, the sheep. Stay with the sheep, Peaches."

Peaches. That made her feel warm. So nice and warm. She just lay there and basked in it.

But soon the warm became hot. Too hot. What was happening? The sheep were nowhere around anymore. Just the heat. A fire. It was burning her.

Natalie forced her eyes open only to find she was surrounded by smoke. She coughed and sat up. Where was she? What was happening?

And why in the world was she outside sitting in half a foot of snow?

"Natalie, stay there." It was Ren again, somewhere nearby but she couldn't see him through the smoke. "There's been an accident."

"A-an accident?" She tried to clear fog from her brain but couldn't.

"Yes, the train derailed or something. Crashed." Suddenly he was there kneeling beside her. She could still barely see him through the smoke, but could see blood streaming over his temple. She coughed again.

"There's a fire." She still couldn't figure out what was going on. "You're bleeding."

"I'm fine. But yes, the train is on fire. You need to stay back. I'm not sure what sort of materials the freight sections were hauling. Could be combustible."

She tried to focus on his words, to understand them, and she did, but it was like they had to wade through mud to get to her brain. She put her hands up to her head.

"Are you okay?"

"My brain is so slow. How did I get here?" She couldn't remember any of it.

"I carried you. I'll tell you the whole story later, okay? But right now I need to go back."

She grabbed his wrists. The thought of him leaving her alone in the dark and smoke and snow, when she couldn't process anything, scared her.

"Am I hurt?" she asked. "I can't seem to figure things out. I feel almost drunk."

"Maybe you hit your head. But I've got to get back in there."

It finally became clear to her. "Oh, my God, the other people. I'll help you." She tried to stand up but dizziness assaulted her.

Ren's hand fell on her shoulder. "No, you

just stay here. Trust me, in the shape you're in, you'll do more harm than good."

"But that elderly lady…"

He gave a curt shake of his head. "She's gone, Peaches. She and the guy who was hitting on you. The way the train car flipped when we derailed…if I hadn't changed spots with the guy it would've been me dead. No one could've survived."

Natalie bit back a sob. "Oh, no."

"Just stay here, okay? I'm going to see if I can find the train engineers, although, honestly, I'm not holding out much hope. But just don't move. We're not far from a ravine, and I don't want you falling. Plus, it'll just put us both in more danger if I have to look out for you, too."

He was right. She couldn't even stand up on her own. "Okay. Be careful."

She felt like he was gone for hours, although she knew it couldn't be more than a few minutes. She was shivering and clenched her jaw as her teeth started chattering. Her stomach revolted every time she moved. She touched all around her head gingerly to see if she could find any lumps that would signify some sort of concussion, but couldn't find anything.

How the hell did someone just sleep through a train crash that killed at least two people?

She remembered dreaming about sheep. About feeling like she was being carried and hearing Ren's voice. Had that been after the crash? When he was getting her out?

Her brain just felt so sluggish. She knew sitting in the snow wasn't helping—physically or mentally—but was afraid to move in case she couldn't find Ren again. The dark and smoke just seemed so all-encompassing. And until her brain started working again, she didn't want to be alone.

But Ren had already been bleeding before he went back to try to help the train engineers. What if he was hurt worse than she thought? What if he was trapped somewhere right now and couldn't get out without help?

She couldn't sit here and do nothing.

She took a few steps into the smoke, coughing as it became thicker. The fire seemed to be getting louder.

"Ren?" she yelled between coughs. "Where are you? Let me help!"

She couldn't hear or see anything. The smoke was too thick.

"Ren!"

Which way should she go? She took a few steps in the direction of what she thought would be the front of the train and where he had headed but she couldn't be sure.

"Natalie!" She'd only gotten a few more steps before she heard him behind her. She turned and ran back in the direction she'd come, arms in front of her in the smoke.

"Ren. I'm here!"

She felt his arms come around her. "Thank God," he whispered against her hair. "I didn't know where you were."

"I couldn't just stay and do nothing. I was worried you might be hurt." She reached up and touched the blood that had dried on his temple.

He kept one arm around her as he led her farther away. "I'm fine. But we've got to get out of here. There's definitely some explosive materials, not to mention we're going to have to find some shelter."

"Is everybody..." She couldn't bring herself to say it.

"They are. I'm sorry, Natalie. It looks like everyone was killed in the initial impact. Somehow we both made it, but we're going to have to get moving if we're going to keep it that way. We've got to go. Right now."

He pulled her, half walking, half running, before wrapping his arm around her and leading them into darkness. She had no idea where they were going, but Ren was determined to get them away from where they'd been.

She understood why a few moments later when a loud fireball burst behind them. Natalie let out a little shriek and fell forward, only saved from falling face-first into the snow by his arm around her.

"Oh, my gosh, was that the train?" She could finally see him a little more clearly now that they were coming out of the smoke.

"Yes, that's why I wanted to get us out of there. But I didn't expect the explosion to be quite that big. Are you okay?"

It was so out of character for her, but she just wanted to lean into him. Into his strength. She didn't know this man at all. Didn't know if he could be trusted. But it didn't stop her from resting her forehead on his chest for just a moment.

They'd almost *died*. Surely it was okay to take just a second and rest here against him.

After a breath she pushed away. She realized he had both her larger backpack and the smaller one.

"I found both your bags—they got thrown from the passenger car. I couldn't find mine, but at least I got my coat."

He set her backpacks on the ground, and Natalie immediately knelt and opened the bigger one, pulling out a dry sweater. No point in putting on dry pants, they were just going to get wet again as they walked.

But at least they were alive. Unlike the others. Tears filled her eyes.

"Hey, you okay?"

"Yeah, I just can't believe this is happening. That everybody's dead and we're not."

He nodded. "I know. Me, too. But we'll have to process it later. Right now survival is the most important thing."

He was right. She would cry for these strangers, but it couldn't be right now. Like he said, survival was the most important thing. That thought helped cut through the fog in her brain a little more.

Survival.

She had been doing that for six years. She had survived everything Damien had done to her, and she would survive this crash. That was what Natalie did: *survive.*

Already, she felt a little better, a little clearer, a little stronger. She clenched her jaw against the chattering of her teeth.

"You're right. Survival is the most important thing." She began digging through the backpack again.

"I don't guess you have hiking boots in there?" Ren asked.

"No, only the tennis shoes on my feet."

"Yeah, me, too. But that's better than nothing. Get as warm as you can, and if you've got an extra sweater to wrap around your head, that will help, too. The body loses a lot of its heat from the head. I have an extra pair of gloves, so use those."

She did as he suggested and handed him a second sweater. He looked a little surprised before taking it and wrapping it around his own head.

"Thanks."

"Do you know where we are?" she asked. "I have no idea what state we're even in."

"I've taken this trip a few times, and based on how long we've been traveling since our stop, I'd put us just over the Utah/Colorado line. But it doesn't matter what state we're in. Either way we're high altitude and not near anything. This was the worst possible place this could've happened."

"Should we stay near the train? Won't someone come looking for us?"

He gave her the smaller backpack and put the larger one on himself. "Eventually they'll come when we don't show up at our next scheduled stop. But that is more than eighteen hours from now. Then by the time they figure out something's actually wrong and get someone out here…we'll die from exposure."

"Oh." Natalie fought not to get overwhelmed. One hour at a time. She just needed to take it one hour at a time.

And at least she was in absolutely no danger from Damien up here. That thought made her smile.

"Want to share your happy thoughts?" Ren tapped the corner of her lips. "I wouldn't mind a little good news."

"Nothing. We're alive. That's what matters. But I guess I shouldn't be smiling."

He pinched the tip of her chin gently. "No, it's okay to smile. We *are* alive. Let's just keep it that way. We need to find shelter for tonight and we'll take stock of everything tomorrow. Food. Water. Figure out a plan."

"Okay. I have a sleeping bag, some protein bars and a water filtering system."

"You do?" Incredulity painted his tone. "Were you on your way to a camping trip or something?"

Yeah, explaining camping equipment when she had no clothes that could be used for that type of activity wasn't easy. "I was sort of relocating and had this stuff in my bag."

"It'll definitely come in handy. Let's get going."

Natalie took a couple steps, then had to stop as dizziness assailed her again.

"You all right?"

"Yeah. I must have hit my head in the crash, although nothing feels tender. I'm just woozy."

He began to walk again, but kept her close to him as they moved. "Shock. Altitude. Cold. A lot of things could be affecting you. And yeah, I'm sure we'll both be totally sore tomorrow."

"Better sore than dead."

She felt his arm tighten around her waist. "Always."

Chapter Six

Ren led them, in a slightly roundabout way, to the overhang he'd found when setting up for this operation last week. He and the team had cleaned it out—not wanting to accidentally find themselves bitten or attacked by something—then carefully made it look as if it had been undisturbed.

Not that Natalie would notice. He didn't think she would notice if there was a couch and television in the small cave. The drugs he'd given her, a tiny injection once she'd fallen asleep to make sure she wasn't conscious when the train "crashed," had affected her a little more than expected. She still seemed woozy and confused, clinging to him a lot more than he suspected she normally would.

Ren would continue to foster that closeness as long as he could. Maybe by the time the drug was completely out of her system her body would already be used to his nearness somewhat. The closer he could get to her, the more information he'd be able to glean.

He'd planned on wrapping the both of them within his coat inside the little cave. That, along with the random pieces of dry timber he and the team had placed inside that would allow him to make a fire, would've made for an uncomfortable but not miserable night.

She had a damn sleeping bag. She'd definitely caught him off guard with that one. Were she and Freihof planning to go on the run, *literally*, where they would need camping gear? A water purifier? Who carried that around if they didn't plan to use it?

Of course, she'd also had stuff that made no sense if she was going somewhere on foot. Paints and brushes. He'd just left them in the bag.

They stepped in a particularly deep drift of snow and it came past her knees. Natalie stiffened almost to the point where her back was bowing. Ren looked over in concern.

"Natalie, what's wrong? Are you hurt?" The drug shouldn't be causing a reaction like this. She looked like she was in pain. Not just pain, but complete agony.

"I just… The snow hurts. It hurts." Her voice sounded odd. Distant. "Please. I'm sorry. I'll be good, just let me out of the snow. It hurts."

What the hell?

He pulled her a few steps forward until she was out of the drift, trying to figure out what was going on. He'd been monitoring their time in the snow, knowing frostbite was a possibility, especially in tennis shoes. But they hadn't been walking long enough for it to be an issue—it shouldn't be causing her pain. She hadn't said anything about it until the drift.

He ripped off his gloves and grabbed his phone to turn on the flashlight. He leaned Natalie—who still looked dazed and frightened—against a tree. Lifting her foot, he checked for any holes in her shoes that he hadn't known about or some sort of wound that had caused her such distress. She was still breathing so deeply she was in danger of hyperventilating.

There was nothing on either her leg or foot that should be causing her pain. And while she was cold, she definitely wasn't anywhere near numbness or frostbite.

He shifted the light back up to look her in the face. Her lips were pinched with pain, her eyes closed. "No more snow. Please, no more snow. I was wrong. You were right."

"Natalie." He put his hands on either side of the sweater she'd wrapped around her head. "Tell me what's wrong."

"No more. It burns so bad. Please," she whispered. Tears were streaming out of her eyes.

Ren didn't know exactly what was happening, but he knew it wasn't part of his plan. They weren't far from the cave so he whisked her up in his arms and cradled her against his chest.

"Okay, Peaches, no more snow. I've got you now. You're not in it anymore."

Her arms came up to wrap around his shoulders, and he pulled her more tightly against himself and farther from the ground. He began walking quickly toward the cave.

Was this some sort of weird phobia? Maybe just a reaction to stress? After all, she thought five other people had died tonight and they'd narrowly escaped with their lives.

She definitely didn't know that if she'd taken another couple dozen steps toward the train when she'd decided to come help him with the "rescue" that she would've seen Ren talking to Philip and Madeline, both very much alive. The three-member train crew? Also totally unharmed.

As a matter of fact, if she'd come out of the circle of smoke, she would've seen the train hadn't crashed at all. It was all a very elaborate smoke and light show. One car had been burning so she could feel the heat, and be scared enough not to come closer.

Damned if she hadn't come anyway, trying to help. Ren had barely caught her in time.

After blowing the carefully laid explosives once he'd given them the signal through a single text, the rest of the team had left and were probably already down in Riverton, the Colorado town that was only about six miles away.

Ren just hoped he didn't have to bring them immediately back up here because Natalie was having some sort of nervous breakdown or allergic reaction to the drugs. The first he could possibly still use to his advantage as long as it didn't get too murky. But the second would require immediate medical attention, effectively bringing the mission to a halt.

She still had her arms wrapped tightly around his neck, trying to hold as much of her own weight as she could, as if that was very significant to begin with. He'd regularly carried more weight for much longer in the special forces. Ren just kept her close and moved quickly toward the cave.

"Here we are, Peaches," he said. He set her down inside the overhang that sheltered them from the wind on three sides. He'd planned to make a big production of searching it to make sure it was safe, but she seemed much more concerned about the white stuff on the ground outside than she did about anything else. He clicked his phone flashlight back on to make sure nothing had taken residence in the last few days.

"Yeah, this will be good," he continued. "Get us out of the elements so we can get some sleep."

She looked around, slowly taking everything in, one of her hands still grasping his shoulder.

"See?" He took the sweater covering her head and pushed it down slightly so she had more freedom of movement of her head. Strands of her light blond hair flew everywhere. "No snow in here. Do you think you can crawl in?"

She nodded and let go of him to slide inside. He took off her backpack and pushed it toward her. She wrapped her arms around it and pulled it up to her chest. But at least she had lost that utterly hollow look in her eyes.

"I think there's enough dry wood in here for us to start a fire. It won't be much of anything, but it will be something. Give a little light. Warmth. But there's no snow in here, okay?"

"Okay," she whispered.

He smiled and began building a small fire in the far corner so the smoke would go outward instead of toward them. She was still cradling her backpack.

"You should probably eat one of your protein bars. Your blood sugar is bottoming out, which is making everything much harder on you."

"What about you?"

"I'll have one in the morning, but right now I'm fine."

She nodded. "I'll get out my sleeping bag, too."

"While you're at it, why don't you try your cell phone? I know you said you didn't have a signal before, but you never know, sometimes you can just catch the right spot and find a signal. I've already tried mine but it didn't work."

Maybe she would make it easy and call Freihof right here and now. Omega had provided a cell signal booster to this area and had an agent monitoring the local 911 dispatch. So if Natalie tried to call someone—hopefully Freihof—the call would go through, but a call to 911 would just disconnect.

It was option one in giving her time to contact Damien, and the easiest. He hoped she'd take it.

But she didn't.

"No, that's okay."

Now that the fire was going, their little dwelling was already becoming more comfortable. Ren took the sweater she'd given him and unwrapped it from his head. He tried to keep any annoyance from his voice.

"You don't want to even try? You never know. It's worth a shot."

She just shrugged and took a bite of her protein bar. "No, I don't have a phone."

What? "Not at all? Not even a really cheap one? Even eight-year-olds have a phone these days."

"Nope. Not me."

"Then how do you contact people? Your friends?" Maybe she'd ditched her phone before she left. Damn it, now he wished he hadn't told her his phone had no signal. He could've offered it to her to use to make a call.

"I haven't had one in years. I don't really like talking on one, I guess. And I don't have a lot of friends. I work a lot."

Ren didn't buy it. She either already had a radio-silence plan in place with her ex-husband or she didn't trust Ren and was hiding her phone until she could contact Freihof in private. Omega would intercept that call if it came.

"Wow, that's crazy, but I'll bet it makes your life more peaceful."

"Will your parents worry about you? Your brother? Since your phone won't work?"

"No. I don't check in with them every day. When they hear about the train, they'll worry. But like I said, it will be days before they back-track to where the accident happened. And hopefully we'll be in civilization before then."

She got that worried look on her face again.

"Is there someone who'll be waiting for you?" he asked. "Worrying? Were you going all the way to Saint Louis?"

She shook her head. "No, there's no one who'll be concerned about me for a long time."

He crawled closer as she got the sleeping bag out and began to unzip it. "You should leave it zipped up," he told her. "You'll stay warmer that way."

"No, that means you'll have nothing. We'll share it."

Ren had to tamp down the unexpected plea-sure that bubbled through his system at the thought of lying next to Natalie. His body didn't seem to care that she was probably a criminal and, if her ex-husband had rubbed off on her at all, she'd be able to kill him while he slept without blinking an eye.

No, his body wasn't interested in acknowl-edging that at all.

He distracted himself by getting some of the snow from outside and placing it inside her water bottle—a perk he hadn't planned on having this early, but was willing to take advantage of—so it would be melted and ready for consumption by the morning. He'd had a large water bottle stashed in the cave when they'd cleaned it out, but now they wouldn't have to use it and explain the sudden appearance of clean drinking water.

He helped her spread the jackets out on the ground so they could lie down on those and would be able to pull the sleeping bag over them. It wasn't going to be the Ritz, but it wasn't half bad.

"I'm feeling much better," she said as she settled next to him, close enough for their body heat to help each other.

"Do you want to tell me what the whole snow thing was about?" he asked.

He could feel her stiffen. "It's a long story. I just don't like snow. I've lived in California for six years so it hasn't been an issue. I guess I was just overwhelmed tonight. I still feel so off."

It had been a hell of a lot more than not liking snow, but Ren let it pass. "You'll feel better tomorrow. Let's get some rest."

He didn't say anything else, didn't give her a chance to say anything else. He just slid behind her on top of the jackets and put her between him and the fire. He reached down and pulled the sleeping bag over them both.

There wasn't much room in the cave, even less in their little sleeping pallet. Although they were both on their backs, Ren was pressed up against Natalie from shoulder to knee. Between the warmth, the exhaustion from what had happened and the drugs still in her system, she should've been asleep pretty rapidly. But an hour later, her stiff form announced that she was far from sleep.

"Peaches, what's wrong?"

She got stiffer. "I just…can't… There's so much… What if…"

When she couldn't get any more words out, Ren did what his body had been begging him to do since they'd lain down. He flipped her on her side so she was facing the fire, slid one arm under her so it cradled her head and wrapped the other around her abdomen and pulled her back until she was firmly tucked against his front.

And damned if her body didn't fit perfectly with his. He wanted to groan and curse at the same time.

"You've been through a trauma," he whispered in her ear. "Your body needs rest. I'm not going to let anything happen to you while you're asleep, okay?" He pulled her a little closer to his body. "Anything that's going to try to get to you has to go through me and that's…"

Ren trailed off. She was already asleep.

Chapter Seven

Damien walked from room to room inside the large Santa Barbara beach house.

Natalie—his Natalie—had been here. He breathed the air from the house deep into his lungs, as if he could inhale her very scent. Natalie was alive.

To discover this wondrous news after all this time was nothing short of a miracle. Ironically, he had Omega Sector, the very people he'd been trying to punish for taking his Natalie away in the first place, to thank for the information. Even though Damien's mole inside Omega was gone, he still had one small channel of information open to him that they hadn't found.

It was what had allowed him to discover and obtain the biological warfare canisters. He was sure they'd discover the tiny leak soon, but it didn't matter, because the most important information he could've ever discovered already had been.

Natalie was alive.

He'd gotten the canisters where they'd needed to go, then flew directly to California as soon as Omega agents—his old nemeses Brandon and Andrea—had been brought in to make contact with Natalie. He wasn't sure how long he'd missed them by, but it was long enough. Now he had no idea where Natalie was, again. He'd have to wait for another phone call to trigger more information.

Damien's fingers strolled along the top of the couch, imagining her sitting here with her feet propped up on the table. She'd always been sloppy like that until he'd come along and cared enough about her to teach her proper behavior. How to be the perfect wife.

Their marriage had been perfect, everything either of them could ever want. He'd helped her become a flawless model of what a wife could be and she'd loved him for it.

He wasn't sure exactly what had happened six years ago. Natalie had obviously been hurt—some sort of head trauma that had caused her to forget their marriage. Forget their perfect life together.

Because the alternative—that she'd run from him on purpose—was impossible.

He walked into the master bedroom, straight up to the bed, pulling back the covers. He bent low so he could smell the pillowcases, wanting to catch even the faintest hint of her essence. Did she still wear the perfume he'd picked out for her during their marriage?

He liked the thought of that. Maybe a subconscious urge she'd had that she didn't even understand because of her memory loss. But deep inside, her brain knew, because like her body and her heart it still belonged to him.

He sniffed again, ripping the pillows off the bed and throwing them to the floor when he couldn't smell anything remotely resembling his Natalie.

He stared at the bed. She had slept here. Without him.

Had someone else joined her in it?

Rage rose in him like a savage wave. His teeth clenched as he forced himself to take a calming breath.

If someone had so much as even touched her, that man would die. And she would need to be punished. He didn't enjoy punishing her, of course. That would make him a monster. But he understood the necessity for it. It helped make her perfect. She'd always understood that, too.

He didn't know how long it would be before

he received word of where Natalie was. And he refused to always be a step behind in something this important. So he would take matters into his own hands as he waited.

This house wasn't in Natalie's name, so it belonged to someone else. Damien would find them and have a talk with them about what they knew. Every single thing they knew.

And then he would find the love of his life once more. It would be like they had never been apart.

NATALIE WOKE UP SLOWLY, stretching her arm out above her. She'd dreamed of sheep farms and train crashes and caves and sleeping wrapped in...

"Careful there, Peaches. Don't want you to stretch too far and accidentally elbow me in the nose."

Oh. Sweet. Heaven.

It hadn't been a dream. And she was half-sprawled on top of Ren. The sun had come up and now she could very clearly see those clear green eyes of his staring out at her. He had one arm under his head, propping him up in a lazily delicious sort of way. Hair tousled. Smile charming.

Natalie felt her heart begin thumping harder in her chest. She immediately scooted back away from him. What on earth was she doing—all but lying on top of a man she hardly knew?

But she couldn't deny—despite every reason why this shouldn't be true, and there were *many*—she'd slept the best she'd ever had since the first time she realized her husband was a monster who would cruelly punish her on a whim. Evidently her exhausted mind had had no trouble giving over her trust to an almost total stranger.

But now her mind wasn't exhausted and she wasn't just going to trust blindly. She had way too many scars to ever let that happen again.

She scampered back a little farther, ignoring the pang of loss she felt as his hand fell off her hip.

"Be careful," he said. "The fire is mostly out behind you but it might have enough heat to burn."

She stopped. "I'm sorry I was basically sprawled all over you."

That smile. Sweet mother of chocolate. "No worries. I can think of a number of things worse than waking up with a beautiful woman draped over me."

"Even in a cave?"

His smile faded as if he remembered why they were here. What had happened. "I'll admit, it isn't the best of circumstances. Are you feeling better?"

The fuzziness in her head was gone, she realized, and she didn't have any pain. So not a head injury, or if it was, not a severe one. "I'm feeling pretty great, considering everything."

"Good. Last night you were a little overwhelmed. The crash, of course, and some other stuff."

Snow. She knew he was talking about her reaction to the snow. But there was no way to be able to explain that easily so she wasn't even going to try. "Yeah, I just can't believe those people are dead. Do you have any idea what happened?"

"No. It was so chaotic. When I came to, everything was surrounded by smoke. I happened to hear you moaning, so that's how I got you out. The lady and the guy were... It was already too late for them."

"So what is our plan now?"

"The last thing I checked before we were out of cell tower range was weather. Mostly I was looking at Montana, but I happened to see an overview of here. It's not good. Snow, Natalie. Not quite a blizzard, but bad."

She could feel her teeth clenching. She was just going to have to overcome the snow.

Mind over matter. She had control. Wasn't tied. Wasn't forced. Wouldn't need to beg.

"Natalie?"

Her eyes snapped to his green ones. "Yep. Got it. We have to walk through the snow and I have to not freak out."

"It's just…"

She nodded. "Yep," she said again. "I know. I freaked out a little last night. I won't let it happen again."

"Okay, then we should get on our way. Try to find better shelter than this before worse weather moves in. Or a town. Or cell coverage, or *something*. Are you sure there's no one you need to get in touch with who will be worried about you?"

How did you explain to someone who had multiple people who would be worried if he was a day late that there was literally not one person in the world who cared if Natalie dropped dead right now?

Maybe Olivia, the waitress from the bar who'd asked Natalie to house-sit in her stead, would be worried. But honestly, Olivia had only asked Natalie because she was desperate to find someone who could take her place. In fact, Olivia had to confirm Natalie was actually her name before she'd asked her about house-sitting. Maybe Natalie's bosses would notice, but Natalie got the impression they were constantly surprised when she'd always shown up to work since she insisted on being paid cash, which, to them, said she was a flight risk.

She had spent the last six years not talking to anyone. Trying to make sure no one really noticed her. Obviously she'd been successful. And it pretty much made her pathetic.

"No, no one will miss me. I guess all my people are used to not hearing from me for a while. We'll make it somewhere before they get to the point of worry."

They shared a protein bar, agreeing that they needed to conserve as much as they could once they got moving, and drank some water through the filtered bottle. They scooted out of the cave into the trees and wilderness surrounding them. They both moved in separate directions to use the bathroom, then came back to wrap up as warmly as possible and were soon ready to leave.

Natalie looked at the snow. It was uncomfortable, it was cold, but she wasn't trapped in it. She could get out of it whenever she wanted. She felt much stronger and more in control.

She would be fine as long as she didn't think too hard about the fact that she *couldn't* actually get out of the snow whenever she wanted. There was nowhere else to go.

Focus, Natalie. Mind over matter.

"Which direction are we heading?"

"East." Ren pointed the opposite way from where they'd come last night. "If I'm not mistaken that should take us into a lower altitude and should be the most direct route to civilization and/or cell phone coverage."

Natalie figured he had just as much to lose—more since he had a business and family—as she did, and since she had no idea which direction they should take, his plan sounded as good as any. Plus, if he had plans to hurt her, he certainly could've done it by now.

But he hadn't. The opposite, in fact. It didn't take much to remember the feel of his arms—his whole body—wrapped around her, keeping her safe, warm, protected.

She forced the thought from her mind. "Sounds good. Let's go."

They began walking.

"Just let me know if you need a break, okay?" He looked over his shoulder since he was leading. "Don't let things spiral. If we need to stop, we need to stop. That's not a problem."

She nodded, a little embarrassed that he had to say it. She knew her paranoia, and not just about snow, sometimes got the best of her. Knew her mind was a little broken after what Damien had done to her. All she could do was try to keep everything in check for right now. Just this one minute. She'd survived that way before. She could do it again.

Chapter Eight

Ren wasn't sure exactly what sort of conduct he'd been expecting from Natalie as they walked. Based on last night's behavior, more distress as they'd walked through the wilderness and snow.

It wasn't easy hiking. Even his muscles were complaining, not to mention a couple of his wounds from his special forces days that tended to act up in the cold. But he knew exactly where they were going and how long it would take to get to the hunter's cabin that would be the crux of this entire mission.

If he was like Natalie and didn't know how far they had to go—if they would be able to find shelter before the weather turned worse, and had some sort of snow phobia—he definitely wouldn't be acting the way she had since they'd started walking.

Focused.

She hadn't muttered a single complaint since

they'd left this morning, even though they'd walked for miles. She'd only stopped to drink water and eat a nutrition bar. Every time he'd glanced at her, she was doggedly putting one foot in front of the other.

The weather had been getting steadily worse, and since he knew there was shelter at the end of this little excursion, he'd had her take out the sleeping bag and wrap it around herself. If she insisted one more time that he take a turn with it, he was going to start feeling bad about leading her in circles in the icy wilderness.

"I can't believe it," he finally said as he led them exactly where he'd planned at exactly the time he'd planned it. He stopped staring at the small structure in front of them. Natalie peeked out from behind him and gasped.

"Is that a *house*?"

She made it sound like a ten-bedroom mansion. He chuckled. "I think *house* might be a bit too generous."

She stepped around him, giving him a grin. "It's got walls and a roof. That's a house!"

She beelined to the door, but he caught up to her before she reached it. "Hang on a second, let me check it first."

He grabbed the door and pushed it open. Inside was exactly like it had been when he'd seen it last week. One large room with a small kitchen on one end and a full-size bed in the corner on the opposite side. An old-fashioned metal wood-burning stove sat in the middle of the room with a couch in front of it.

Natalie was already pushing at his back. "Is it safe? What's it like? Please tell me the roof isn't leaking."

He stepped all the way in so she could follow. He expected a bit of disdain for the small, almost barren space, especially given the size of her Santa Barbara beach house, but she surprised him again.

"Is this not the most amazing place you've ever seen?" Her grin was ear to ear.

He shook his head. "You must really be glad to get out of the snow to think this is the best place ever."

She laughed. "Okay, it's not the White House. But what about that stove, right? And it already feels warmer in here."

"That's because the wind is blocked. But yeah, let's see about getting the stove to work."

They checked the two other doors in the room. One led to a large shed, stacked with wood in the back of the cabin, the other to a detached outhouse. Within fifteen minutes, Ren had a fire blazing and the cabin was warm enough that they had to remove their jackets.

Natalie wandered into the kitchen, gasping as she found cans of soup and vegetables in the small pantry.

"What is this place? Obviously it gets used. Are we closer to civilization than we think?"

Ren shook his head. "Actually, probably the opposite. This is a hikers/hunters cabin. For use when people are going to be away on extended trips." He pulled out his phone and made a show of checking it. "Still no signal."

She didn't look nearly as upset as he'd expected her to at the news.

"Well, at least we have shelter and a little food." She began counting and organizing. "Enough for today at least. I'll start dinner, I'm starving."

They worked together in the kitchen, finding what they needed to open the can of vegetable soup and a pot to pour it in. Ren also brought in some snow to heat over the fire so they could have drinking water through her filtration bottle.

"Tomorrow I'll go out and set some traps. See if I can catch us some food. Or there must be a river nearby since there are fishing poles in the corner."

"Do you think a storm is still coming in?"

He nodded. "The heaviness in the air when

it's this cold? Definitely more snow. We might be trapped here for a few days."

He was hoping the thought of being trapped would push her toward wanting to make a call. But he was beginning to believe her when she said she didn't have anyone to call. Maybe she and Freihof had a no-contact pact in situations like this.

Tomorrow he would be checking in with Steve Drackett and needed to have a plan. The problem was, the more time he spent with Natalie, the less confident he was that she was conspiring with her ex.

But he couldn't say for sure. That was the problem.

They ate, not nearly enough to be full, but enough to push away actual hunger pains. Afterward they washed their meager dishes in the faucetless sink with the now-melted snow Ren had brought in. Then Natalie searched the entire cabin and laid out everything that could be eaten, as well as anything that could be used to help them in other ways: tools, knives, the fishing poles.

She hadn't stopped moving since they'd arrived, and that was after they'd already walked nearly ten miles today in the snow. As the sun went down, she'd just gotten more frantic in her activities.

"Hey, Peaches, you want to sit for a while? We've had a long day and you haven't slowed down since the moment we got here." He patted the couch cushion next to him.

She turned from rearranging the supplies—again—and gave him a sheepish grin. "Yeah, sorry, I like to have things in order. Know where stuff is." She looked from the door to the cabin's two windows. "Just in case."

"Just in case what?"

She walked over to the door. "Just in case there's no time to sort through stuff if there's an emergency. Better to be prepared."

"Okay, I think we're suitably prepared. Why don't you take a load off?"

She looked over her shoulder at him. "There's no lock on this door."

"No, there's not supposed to be. This cabin is open for anyone who needs it. We have a number of similar ones throughout Montana. Just for people who maybe get stranded and, of course, people who plan to use it. So, no locks."

"No locks," she whispered. She walked to the windows, checked them also.

Ren stood. What exactly was happening here? "No locks on those, either."

"Right." She gave a little laugh that didn't hold any humor. "Because why would you put locks on a window when you didn't have one on the door?"

"Exactly."

Her back was stiff again, and although she wasn't jumping straight into the deep end of a panic attack like she had with the snow, she was definitely becoming more tense.

"Natalie."

She didn't respond, just kept looking at one window, then the other.

He walked over and put his hands gently on her shoulders. She didn't even jump like he half expected her to. "Natalie. You're tired. Come sit down, okay?"

"It's dark out," she whispered. "I always check the locks. And the sticky notes won't help if there aren't any locks on the doors or windows."

He had no idea what the sticky notes comment was about. He pulled her over to the couch and sat down with her, her hands in his. "You're tired, Peaches."

"I shouldn't be tired. It's still pretty early."

"Are you kidding? We walked for hours, then you made dinner, cleaned up and did your whole inventory of any useful items. You're tired."

She rolled her eyes, giving him the tiniest

smile. "I work longer than this on any given day. I'm sure you do, too, on the farm."

The work she did in Santa Barbara couldn't be as hard as what her body had been through today. But it was a good time to press for details. "I do work hard on the farm when I'm there. What do you do?"

She glanced away. "I'm between jobs at the moment."

"I'll bet you were in business. At an office? I can totally see you as an executive."

"Ha. I wish. No such luck."

He smiled. "A secretary, then? No shame in that."

She tried to slide her hands back from his, but he wouldn't let her. He needed to get her to open up to him. He rubbed his fingers along her palms, trying to calm her, since she kept glancing back to the door and windows.

The texture of her hands didn't register at first. The hardened bumps where her fingers met her palms. When he realized what they were, he stopped his rubbing and turned her hands over.

Her hands had noticeable calluses. Ren recognized them for what they were because he had similar ones on his own palms. They'd been even worse when he'd lived on the farm.

They came from holding a wooden handle

of something in your hands all the time. In his case it had been shovels or brooms, or even the horses' bridles. Days and years of hard work.

He wasn't ashamed of his calluses, and would never think poorly of a woman who had them, either—the opposite, in fact.

But for the life of him he couldn't figure out why Natalie Freihof's hands would have them. He'd watched her for the last week go to office buildings and a bar. Business meetings and parties.

Nothing that should have her hands in this shape.

She looked down at her hand resting in his. "Not so pretty, huh?" Her eyes immediately flew back to the door.

He didn't mention her hands again. He wasn't going to get any info out of her when all she seemed to be able to focus on was the fact that the door wouldn't lock.

It didn't make any more sense than her snow phobia did last night. But he could see she was on the path toward another breakdown.

"Natalie, look at me."

He could tell it cost her effort to look away from the door and meet his eyes, but she did.

"Can I tell you something I've realized about you in the short time I've known you?"

She nodded.

"You're strong. When you thought I might need help at the train, you were coming to do it, even though you were hurt. Today when we had to walk, you did it without complaint. Once we got here, you got to work doing what needed to be done."

"But now I'm freaking out," she whispered. "Just like I did last night. You have to think I'm crazy."

He pulled her closer. "No, I don't. But I do think a body only has so much energy and it can only be utilized so many ways. You're completely exhausted right now, and because of that, your fears about the locks on the doors and windows are overwhelming you. If you weren't so exhausted you'd be able to handle it better, right?"

"Not always, but usually."

"How would you do that?"

She looked away. "I have a method of making sure I've locked the doors and windows. I use sticky notes. It's stupid."

"There's nothing to be ashamed about. You had a problem and you figured out how to work it."

She shrugged. "Doesn't help me much now."

"How about if we pull one of the kitchen chairs over and wedge it under the door handle? It doesn't exactly lock it, but it will be damn loud if someone tries to open it."

Her face was already looking more relaxed, so Ren continued. "We can't lock the windows, but we can close the shutters and put a broom handle across the bars. Again, it's not foolproof but it's definitely more fortified."

The relief that flooded her features was so pronounced it was difficult to look at.

After they'd made the cabin as safe as they could—he noticed she double-checked more than once—they washed and brushed their teeth as best they could and got into bed. Ren tried to ignore the fact that he wished it was colder in the cabin so that they'd be forced to get closer for heat. The bed wasn't that big, but it was bigger than their sleeping arrangements last night.

As he heard Natalie's breathing even out as exhaustion pulled her under, Ren lay for a long time trying to process what he had learned tonight about the woman lying next to him. Unfortunately he had more questions than answers. Questions that would affect every decision Ren made for the rest of this mission.

Why did she have calluses on her hands that suggested she'd been doing hard manual labor every day for years? Why was she fanatic about locking up and safety?

Because she knew that Freihof had a number of enemies who wouldn't hesitate to attack her to get to him?

Or because she was afraid of Freihof himself?

Chapter Nine

Ren woke up to a sleeping Natalie sprawled all over him again. She'd been that way most of the night. It hadn't taken long after she'd finally fallen into an exhausted slumber, secure in the knowledge that the windows and doors were as locked as they could be, before she'd snuggled into him.

He should've pushed her away, rolled over, hell, gone and slept on the couch. Curling her lithe body next to his while they both slept didn't do anything to advance the mission—she was asleep, so it wasn't affecting her. And if their closeness didn't advance the mission, then it shouldn't have interested Ren at all.

But damned if he'd been able to let her go all night.

He eased away from her now as dawn approached. He needed to go out, make the call to Omega, finalize plans.

Plans that were even murkier than they'd

been when they'd started two days ago. Everything he learned about Natalie just made him more confused. He'd been so sure she was working with Freihof. But the calluses on her hands didn't lie.

The fear on her features last night, the panic at the thought of not being able to lock the doors and windows, didn't lie, either.

But none of that gave Ren actionable intel. So he wasn't sure how to play this with her.

Even worse, he wasn't sure he wanted to play this at all. If time wasn't such a factor—with those damned biological warfare canisters—Ren would probably remove himself from the picture entirely. Obviously he was losing his objectivity when it came to her.

He looked down at her sleeping form, how she'd curled protectively into herself, even in sleep. As if her mind knew some sort of attack might be coming.

But from who?

Ren found a pen and paper and wrote that he'd be back soon and laid it on the bed where she would see it. He didn't want her waking up and thinking someone had gotten in the cabin because the door was no longer barred. She might wake up and not be thinking clearly at first.

He wiped a hand across his face as he realized that he wasn't just concerned—*again*—about the damage that might do to the mission. He was concerned about the damage it might do to her psyche.

He had to get his damned head in the game.

Grabbing the knife and fishing poles, he moved quietly out the door and made his way deeper into the forest away from the cabin. He came up to the river a few minutes later and cast a pole with a fly lure—might as well try to catch some protein to go with the canned food—then used a specially made cell signal booster to call Steve Drackett.

"Ren. Good to hear from you. How's camping?"

"We made it to the cave and then the cabin on schedule. Rest of the team make it safely from the crash site?"

"Yep. No problem, although now Philip Carnell is convinced he wants to work undercover full-time."

Ren chuckled. "That would at least get him out of your hair." Philip was known for his surliness and inability to play well with others. "Let him terrorize some criminals instead of your agents."

"Definitely something to consider. How's it going with Natalie? She give you anything useful yet?"

"Honestly, no, nothing. She hasn't panicked about not being able to make contact and wasn't interested in using my phone to try to call anyone."

Steve gave some sort of disgruntled sigh. "So what's your plan? Threats? Friendship? Seduction? Before you choose, there's been some developments you need to know about."

"What?"

"For one, Sean and Theresa Baxter."

"Why do those names sound familiar?" He knew he should be able to place them.

"They were the names on the deed of the Santa Barbara house where Natalie was staying. We were looking into them as a possible front."

"What did you find?" Ren asked.

"They definitely weren't a front. Were actually real-life people who legitimately purchased the house in 2003."

Ren didn't like how Steve was phrasing this. *"Were?"*

"They were both found murdered at a resort bungalow in Puerto Vallarta, Mexico, last night. Brutally. Tortured."

Ren's curse was nothing short of foul. Just when he thought he was closer to getting a handle on things. "What the hell does that mean, Steve? Tying up loose ends? An enemy of Freihof's trying to get information?"

Could Natalie have ordered their deaths before she left to make sure they wouldn't be able to tell anyone anything about her? Not just killed, but tortured?

"We've been running info on the Baxters all night and haven't found anything to suggest they were linked to Freihof or Natalie in any way. Nothing."

"Which we both know doesn't necessarily mean anything. Not with a criminal of Freihof's caliber."

"True," Steve replied before they both dropped into silence. "So what's your plan?" Steve repeated.

"Until what you just told me, I was beginning to think that Natalie might be completely innocent in all this. A victim, like Brandon and Andrea said."

"But we can't deny that no one knew she was running except us and her. No one would know to tie up loose ends like the Baxters."

"Exactly. Plus, Lillian said Natalie mentioned Atlanta when she was trying to buy a bus ticket. That can't be a coincidence that it's Freihof's last known whereabouts." Ren ran a hand over his face. "Did you discover anything new about those office buildings she went to every day? That bar?"

"As far as we can tell, all the companies in both buildings are clean. Maybe some minor tax stuff, but nothing that would put them on any radars. If Natalie was using one as a front, she was damn good at it. And the bar has been family-owned for generations. I have no idea what she was doing there."

Ren thought of the calluses on her hands again. He didn't know, either. And he was afraid the truth was going to make this mission even less simple.

"What does your gut say about her, Ren?" Steve finally asked when he didn't say anything. "You and I have been in the spy game for a long time. I would take your gut instinct over some incomplete intel any day."

What did his gut say? His gut said he was already too compromised to make an impartial judgment when it came to Natalie. That every time he looked into those endless blue eyes, it seemed impossible that she could be mixed up with Freihof. That she couldn't be a killer or be collaborating with someone who was.

But his gut also told him that those baby-blues, that tragic smile, even the panic, could all be part of a very specific ploy to fool him. That she could've been trained by Freihof for years on how to best manipulate a law enforcement agent. God knew there was no better teacher than Freihof when it came to exploitation.

"My gut says I need more time," he finally told Steve. "I need to be able to dig deeper into her and pick her apart."

"We don't have a lot of time. There's been another development."

Not what Ren wanted to hear. "What?"

"Because of the canisters, Homeland Security is breathing down my neck. They want to assume control of the op and take Natalie into custody."

"You know if they do that she'll be treated like a hostile subject and terrorist enemy of the United States." It would be illegal to torture her, but that didn't mean they couldn't make her incarcerated time extremely uncomfortable. "We don't have enough intel yet to even suggest she's guilty or knows anything about Freihof."

"That's what I told them and convinced them that you getting her cooperation voluntarily would be not only more efficient, but humane. Especially if she really is innocent in all this."

"How long can you hold them off?"

"Five days at the max, Ren. And that's with

calling in every favor I have. If you don't walk into Riverton in five days, they're coming in to take her."

"And if I come out with no answers but Natalie's agreement to cooperate with the media blitz plan?"

"They don't like it," Steve said. "But they've agreed. As long as we're taking measurable steps forward."

A fish bit at one of the fishing lines and Ren leaned down to reel it in, but it had gotten away. Fitting. "Do you have everything set on your end for when we come out five days from now?"

"Yes. We'll have every major news outlet waiting in Riverton to cover the huge story of two lost hikers finding their way out of the wilderness. That tiny Colorado town will be packed with media, I promise. We'll spin the romance angle. It'll work."

Ren recast the line back out into the stream. "It's got to be big. Big enough for Freihof to hear about it wherever he is. If she doesn't know where he is, this will get him to come to us."

"Barring some international incident the news has to cover, we'll make sure this is top priority. That it goes viral. But, Ren, it won't work if she comes out all angry and refuses to get in front of the camera."

"She won't. I'll get her cooperation." He said it with a great deal more assurance than he felt.

"Like, you know, Brandon and Andrea both think she's innocent. They think that if you're honest with her, tell her about the canisters and what Freihof could do with them, that she'll help you."

Ren wanted to believe it. But he also knew that if he believed it and he was wrong, a lot of innocent people would die. Like it or not, Natalie was their best chance to catch Freihof, either by her telling them how he could be located or by using her as bait to draw him out.

"You've got five days to figure out the best way to use her," Steve continued.

Ren couldn't help his wince at the word *use*, even though he knew Steve was right. The softness of the woman he'd held in his arms the last two nights was secondary to what she could provide as an asset. Ren had to steel himself against any sort of tenderness toward her.

That was what he was known for, right? Getting the job done. Getting what he needed by any means necessary. Feelings had nothing to do with stopping a killer.

Ren could feel the darkness, the shadows

he'd lived and fought in for so long, wrap around him a little more tightly. Another little piece of his soul gone.

"Five days," he said to Steve. "I'll have what we need. Just be ready."

The sound of cracking branches in the distance had him turning and slipping the phone into his jacket pocket. A few moments later Natalie came into view.

"Hi." She rushed in, then stopped, breathing a little hard. She was back in her jeans and sweater, the sleeping bag wrapped around her again. She looked around, then took a few steps closer. "I just wanted to make sure everything was okay. And then it sounded like you were talking to someone and I got excited."

Damn it. "I was talking to someone." He smiled, then jerked his head toward the river. "This damn fish. Trying to coerce him onto my hook."

Ren swallowed a curse as her eyes narrowed like she didn't quite believe him. He let go of the rod and closed the distance between them until they were only a couple of feet from each other.

"I thought you'd sleep longer and not witness the lunacy that runs in my family in the form of talking to fish."

"I'm normally an early riser." She looked at

the river, then back at him. "You were really talking to the fish?"

How much had she heard? "Did you hear what I was saying?"

"No."

He stepped closer. He had to get her mind off this, and there was only one way he knew how. "I was telling the fish I needed to catch him so I could take him back to the beautiful woman I found draped over my body again this morning."

"I was?" That flush. Damn, it was so adorable.

He reached out and grabbed the edges of the sleeping bag, pulling her closer. "You were. And just like yesterday I didn't mind it at all."

"I'm sorry. I don't know why I keep doing that… I just— I mean…"

He brought his lips down to hers, stopping her words.

The kiss was supposed to be a distraction. A way to stop her thinking about having heard him talking. Light. Fun. Hint of sweet flirtation and possible promise of more.

But the moment their lips touched every agenda he had vanished. What he meant to be sweet and soft immediately turned heated. Scorched air filled his lungs as she gave a little gasp at the attraction that crackled and danced around them.

He took complete possession of her mouth. There was no other word for it. His fingers slipped from the grip he had on the sleeping bag to slide around her back, wrapping low around her hips. The fingers of his other hand wound into the hair at the base of her neck, anchoring her in place so he could kiss her more deeply.

And he did. Over and over. Taking her mouth with a need he hadn't even known could exist, especially not in a situation like this. He moved her back against a large tree, pulling her closer as her arms entwined around his neck.

It was her soft sigh of something close to wonder that brought him back to reality.

What the hell was he doing? That kiss had left the distracting-her-from-almost-catching-him category within the first three seconds and had gone straight to…

Hell if he knew.

He stepped back, giving him some much needed distance, and found her clear blue eyes blinking up at him as if she couldn't quite figure out what was going on.

Know the feeling, Peaches.

He gave her a smile and moved away, trying—way too late—to make this more casual. And fighting the fear that this was going to leave them both bloody in the end.

Chapter Ten

Ren was showing her how to clean a fish.

Definitely not very romantic—although more romantic than teaching her how to skin the rabbit they'd caught a few hours ago—and yet, Natalie couldn't deny the closeness between them. An easiness that almost bordered on fun, which was crazy since they were lost in the middle of the wilderness.

But for her, not crazy at all. Not since she woke up this morning and realized she had nothing to fear out here.

Okay, maybe wild animals and blizzards. She could handle those. But the fear that she would turn around and possibly find Damien standing there was gone. For the first time she was one hundred percent certain he had no idea where she was.

Hell, *she* had no idea where she was. How could Damien possibly find her?

He couldn't.

That was the truth she'd come to grips with this morning. And that left Natalie with a feeling of freedom she hadn't known for as long as she could remember. A sense that anything was possible, even if she did have to learn to catch and cook her own meat in order to supplement what they had inside the cabin.

And then there was Ren.

If she had to be trapped in the wilderness, she couldn't have picked a better person to be trapped with. He knew how to hunt, fish, clean and prepare food.

And kiss.

That kiss. It hadn't been far from her mind since this morning.

She'd *never* been kissed like that. Not even before Damien had become a vicious monster. Never been kissed like someone wanted her more than he wanted his next breath. Like he might forget they were in the middle of the frozen wilderness and take her right there against the tree.

And Natalie was pretty sure she wouldn't have stopped him. Especially considering she hadn't even been able to remember her own name at that moment, had only been able to *feel*.

He hadn't kissed her again. Hadn't really touched her, except as needed when they were hunting and fishing. She would almost think she'd imagined the whole thing if it wasn't for the slight tenderness of her lips because of the onslaught from his.

"You ready to chop the head off?"

His words yanked her back. She made a face.

He smiled, rolling those green eyes. "You did pretty well earlier. I would think a fish would be easier."

"I was hungrier earlier." And the meat had been delicious. But she took the hatchet from him and quickly lopped off the head of the fish like he'd shown her and they began to clean it together.

Although she didn't particularly like doing *this*, providing for herself gave her a sense of accomplishment. Purpose. A couple of hours later they had a fish broth with canned potatoes. And damned if it wasn't one of the best meals she'd ever eaten. Because she'd been responsible for it herself.

After a lifetime of never being good enough at anything, some fish broth made by her own hands felt pretty fantastically rewarding.

"Did you do a lot of hunting and fishing on your farm?" she asked as they washed the dishes.

He looked at her for a long moment, as if

he needed to decide something. He closed his eyes, tensing, and she hated that she had broken the easiness that had been between them all day by sticking her nose where it didn't belong.

"I'm sorry," she began. "I—"

"Actually, I learned most of my hunting tricks in the military. It was part of the wilderness and survival training I did during my time in the special forces."

She folded the towel in her hand slowly and hung it on the rack. "Oh, wow. I didn't know you'd been in the... I'm not sure which branch is special forces."

"In this case, army," he said. "I love the farm. Love my family. But I wanted to get out. See the world. See what else I was capable of."

That made sense. He had a quiet, understated strength and confidence about him that would've been honed in the military, much more than it ever would've been on a farm.

"Did you like it? Why did you get out?"

"I was good at it. But I liked being my own boss, not having to follow orders blindly. So I got out after six years."

She smiled as he gestured toward the living room, and they took a seat on the couch. "Did you get to see the world like you wanted?"

"I did. All over the place. The only continent

I didn't make it to was Antarctica. I have this huge collection of postcards from all these different places sitting in a box at home."

"You didn't mail them to anyone?"

He smiled and it caused a bloom of warmth in her chest. Near her heart. "Some to my mom, but no, mostly I just collected them. Never really had someone I cared about enough to want to share my life with. How about you, ever married?"

The warmth immediately froze. It wasn't an unreasonable question. Funny, last week she wouldn't have even known how to answer without knowing if she was lying. Brandon and Andrea had at least given her that truth. "Um, yeah. Once. A while ago. It ended."

"I'm sorry."

She wasn't. "Some things die. Aren't meant to survive. Better just to let it stay buried."

How badly she wished she could let her marriage be buried. To put it truly behind her with no hold on her anymore.

Thankfully, Ren changed the subject. "So, you said you're between jobs. Relocating. To Saint Louis?"

"No." God, how much should she tell him? She didn't want to lie to Ren since he'd been so friendly, but if those Omega Sector people came to question him, she didn't want him to have any information. She would give him what she could without any specifics. "Honestly, I'm not sure. It was just time for a change. I'll get a job when I get to wherever I'm going."

"And what kind of job will that be?"

The same as before, she guessed. Whatever she could get being paid under the table. Dishwashing, cleaning, maybe lawn work. She shrugged. "Whatever I can get. I'm not really picky."

He smiled again, stretching his arm along the back of the couch, and her heart tripped over its own beat. "Not trying to become a millionaire?"

"No, money's not important to me."

"You sound pretty sure about that."

That was one of the few things she could say with absolute certainty. "Oh, I am. Some of the years when I was surrounded by the most money—a huge house, fancy cars and meals—were the most miserable I'd ever been in my whole life."

His fingers tucked a strand of her hair behind her ear. "I'm sorry to hear that."

"I always wanted to travel places, like you did. But…my ex-husband had other interests."

Ren shifted closer. "What sort of interests?"

She shrugged. To this day she still didn't know much about Damien or what he did business-wise. She knew he'd stolen money, and that was how he'd become rich, but by the time she'd figured that out she'd been too deep in his clutches for it to make a difference.

"His work."

"Was that bad? What did he do?"

She shifted in her seat. "I know this sounds so stupid, but I really don't know every pie he had his fingers in. I never did. I married him really young. I lost both my parents when I was eighteen and didn't have any other family. I was sort of lost. He swept into the art studio where I was working, made me feel like the most talented and important person in the world, then married me six weeks later."

And put her in a cast six months after that.

"He never traveled with you anywhere? Even with all that money?"

Not after he decided she flirted with everyone she came in contact with and that she needed to be kept apart from everyone else. Once he decided he would make her perfect.

She'd never been perfect enough. "No. He had his own priorities."

"Sounds like he wasn't any good for you and you should be glad the marriage is over."

Oh, she was. She just wasn't sure Damien would feel the same way if he knew she was alive.

"What?" Ren asked. "What was that look?"

She wanted to trust him with the whole story, tell him how she'd faked her death and was afraid Damien would find her and hurt her again. She'd carried this for so long alone. The fear, the exhaustion, the isolation.

But it wasn't Ren's burden to carry.

So she just smiled. "No look. Things just don't turn out like you thought they would, sometimes."

His green eyes studied hers. "I know."

She leaned her head back against the couch, against his hand still resting there.

"You ready to learn how to use the flint and make some fire with no matches?" he finally asked. It was one of the things he promised to show her. "The fire is down enough that I'll put it out and you can rebuild it. It'll be part of your SERE training."

She laughed, sitting up with him. "My what?"

"SERE. Survival, Evasion, Resistance and Escape. It's a military acronym for training they give us."

"I'm really only getting the S, so I don't know if the army would approve."

He chuckled. "Probably true. Let's hope you never need the other, anyway, seeing as it was a carry-over from soldiers who escaped and evaded Nazis in World War II."

"Yeah, I'm hoping not to be evading Nazis any time soon."

He showed her how to build kindling starting with the smallest and finest twigs she could find. When she had what looked like a tiny teepee in the stove belly, he stepped back.

"Okay, strike the steel against the flint like I showed you, close to the tinder, and you'll be all set."

He stood up behind her. Natalie stared down at the round piece of steel—it looked like it belonged on the bridle of a horse—in one hand and the flint, which looked like a plain rock you might find in any backyard, in the other.

She tried to get it to work, but couldn't. How hard could it be? Hitting one hard object against the other, getting a little spark and starting a fire? It certainly hadn't looked difficult when Ren had shown her.

Tension began strumming through her as she continued to try. Her aggravation was doubled by knowing Ren was watching this whole time, probably wondering why she was so inept. Tears stung her eyes at her inability to get such a simple task completed. He'd shown her more than once, given her understandable instructions, and she couldn't get it.

After another few minutes, sweat now dripping across her brow, she saw one of his shoes come into her line of vision as he moved closer. She forced her arms to hit the flint harder, even though she was tired now and holding herself in this position was hurting her back.

How long before he lost his patience and started yelling? Or just pushed her out of the way and did it himself?

"Natalie."

She waited for the belittlement.

"Take a breath, okay, Peaches?"

She hunched her shoulders. "I can't do it. I'm sorry."

A moment later he was crouched behind her. "No need to be sorry. It can be tricky to use flint the first time." His arms came around her, his hand covering hers on the steel and stone. "Try hitting it at a slightly steeper angle."

He showed her again so she could get the feel for the motion. Then he let go, putting his hands on the stove, keeping her fenced between his arms. After a few more times she struck it again, and this time it worked.

Ren's hands trailed up her arms to her shoulders as he moved away from her. "See? Just needed to get a feel for it. Nobody gets everything perfect all the time."

Natalie looked away. When she thought about all the times she'd been *corrected* by

Damien for not doing something right…which had usually involved his fists or worse. He'd demanded that she be perfect. Always perfect. In her life. In her art.

She never was.

"Whoa, hey, what's going on here?" He reached over and cupped her cheeks, wiping tears with his thumbs. "There's no crying in SERE training."

She tried to smile. "I couldn't get it. It wasn't right."

"Are you kidding? You've now built a fire that's so big we're going to have to crack a window."

"But…"

"Natalie, you did it. That's what matters. And hell, even if you hadn't been able to do it, you could've tried again tomorrow."

There had never been *try again tomorrows* with Damien. Only pain.

The urge to run now was strong. She needed to get away even from Ren, who'd never been anything but kind. Knowledge that she didn't have anywhere to go had panic lacing her veins.

"I—I need to go to the bathroom."

She flung herself by him and through the

door that led to the attached outhouse. She had to pull herself together.

Ren was right. Perfection was not required here. Who cared if she couldn't get the fire started? Ren certainly hadn't. And more importantly, she *had* gotten it started.

She'd had such a peace this morning at the knowledge that Damien couldn't find her here. It wouldn't last forever; they'd have to leave soon—if not tomorrow, then in a few days, tops. She'd probably never have another place where she'd feel so secure again.

She wouldn't let the ghost of Damien past ruin her present.

Since she was there she used the bathroom, then walked back into the cabin. She expected to find Ren with eyes full of questions she wasn't sure she was going to know how to answer.

Instead, at first she didn't see him at all. Then he straightened himself from where he'd obviously been putting something on the ground near the wall at the other end of the room, by the front door.

He held his hands out in front of him in a gesture of peace. "Look, I wasn't snooping, but this morning I was looking through your backpack, trying to see if there was anything in there that could be useful, that you might have missed in the inventory you did yesterday."

She nodded. There wasn't anything she was hiding in the bag. "I don't really have anything."

"You have these." He motioned for her to come forward. After a few steps she could see what he'd laid out on the floor.

Her paints.

"I saw them this morning, but I didn't know if they were yours. Then a few minutes ago you mentioned working at an art studio so then I thought…"

She couldn't stop staring at them.

"Are they not yours?" he finally asked.

"No, they are. It's just—it's just… It's been a long time since I've used them. I've been carrying them around, but never used them."

"How about now?"

Her eyes flew to his face. "Now? Where? I don't have any canvas."

"I thought maybe a section of that door could be your canvas. You could give the owners of this cabin a nice surprise. And if they don't like it, it'll take them ten minutes to sand it down."

"But…"

He smiled, handing her a brush. "It doesn't have to be perfect."

She took the brush. It was time to take back part of what had been stolen from her.

Chapter Eleven

He awoke to the sound of Natalie's adorable snores against his neck.

This was the third day in a row he'd woken up to the feel of her in his arms. This morning she had a leg thrown over his hips and her arm wrapped around his stomach as she'd plastered herself to his side. Unlike the other two nights, she'd been completely relaxed all night. And although she hadn't started out in his arms, she'd certainly ended up there quickly. Not that Ren was complaining.

Although he was not complaining for the wrong reasons.

He should be happy that she was finally relaxed enough to roll into his arms because it meant she was getting closer to trusting him. Not because she felt damn near perfect in his arms.

He'd watched her paint for hours last night until she'd been too tired to hold her arms up against the door that had become her small masterpiece.

Had a hundred-dollar set of paints been the key to cracking Natalie from the beginning?

After watching her for a few hours, Ren was sure he could've saved a whole lot of time and money by just showing up at her door in Santa Barbara with an easel and encouraged her to do her best.

He wasn't sure why no information about Natalie as an artist had been in her Omega file. But the more she worked on the painting, the more evident her talent became. Like professionally good.

The sheer joy on her features as she worked—the utter serenity—was so intense it had been impossible for Ren to look away. Like she'd been waiting an unimaginable amount of time to do this, and then couldn't stop if she wanted to. And she very definitely hadn't wanted to.

Last night, painting by firelight, Natalie was almost the polar opposite of the woman who'd been frantically searching for a way to lock windows and doors with no locks the night before. She was serene, calm and utterly beautiful.

Actually, most of yesterday had been different. Except for the incident starting the fire, she'd been relaxed and helpful. She'd surprised him by wanting to learn how to hunt and how to prepare the animals to eat. Then surprised him even more at being so deft at it.

The more she did, the more he wanted to show her. The more they talked, the more truths he told. When he'd told her about his time in the special forces he knew he was in dangerous territory. But more and more he was finding it impossible to believe that she could be in with Freihof.

And if she wasn't, if there was nothing she could tell him about Freihof's location, then Ren knew he needed to end this. Tell her who he was, what was happening, and ask for her help. Lay all the cards out, talk her into helping, pack them up and leave.

He looked over at her painting taking up about one quarter of the cabin door. She'd be done by the end of today at the rate she was going. He'd let her finish. Partially because doing so would hopefully make her more agreeable to helping them hunt her ex-husband. But mostly because he couldn't stand to cut short the use of those paints that had brought such life to her so-often-haunted eyes.

He'd try to get more information from her today as she painted and was more relaxed. Maybe she knew something she wasn't aware of. Details that weren't important to her, but could be used for finding and stopping Freihof.

But one thing Ren knew for sure was that he needed to distance himself from her. Because, yeah, she was going to be mad when she found out he'd been deceiving her all this time. If he fostered any more closeness, it would just make the situation that much more difficult.

Natalie shifted slightly from where she was draped over him. He closed his eyes as her body squeezed more tightly up against him.

He needed distance just as much for his own sake as hers. Especially since he was the one who was undercover; and yet he was finding it almost impossible to lie to her.

For someone who had made a career out of lying to others, giving them whatever false information and security they needed in order to get what he wanted, not being able to lie to this woman was downright disconcerting.

Or maybe it wasn't that he *couldn't* lie to her, it was that he didn't want to. Just about everything he'd told her except for his last name—and even then, Thompson was his mother's maiden name—had been true. Telling her about his time in the special forces? Completely unnecessary. And yet…he hadn't regretted telling her.

He wanted her to know him. And when he

asked questions, yes, he was always listening for potential info about Freihof, but he was also getting to know her.

And was liking it.

Which was possibly the most dangerous thing he could do. Especially given that nuclear kiss yesterday morning.

Distance. It was the best tactical move he could make right now. He eased himself out from under her—ignoring his body's demands that he stay exactly where he was—and got out of the bed.

He needed distance.

NATALIE COULD HONESTLY say she'd never seen a door be used as an actual canvas before. Her face broke out into a grin as she leaned back in to complete the section she was working on. Who cared if it was untraditional, if the paint soaked in more than it would on canvas? It still worked.

And she was painting. It had been years since she'd held a brush. Since she'd felt the calm flow through her body that she only got when painting.

She was painting the view of the Pacific from the beach house. It was an unusual choice for a cabin in a landlocked state, particularly in the middle of winter, but she liked to think the owners would come and be surprised and like it.

Although they couldn't possibly like looking at it as much as she'd liked painting it. She'd started again as soon as she'd woken up this morning, after eating the breakfast Ren had already graciously fixed, and had been at it most of the day. She'd only stopped when her arms or back—unused to this type of abuse since it had been so long since she'd painted—had begun to protest too loudly.

She painted in another section of blue that morphed into teal. The colors blended beautifully in front of her, the image from her mind taking formation on the wood. This was what she was meant to do. Had always been what she'd been meant to do.

She couldn't believe she'd allowed this to be stolen from her for so many years. During her marriage—when none of her paintings had ever been perfect enough for Damien—but then also after. She'd been so busy making sure she was ready to run, able to hide, that she'd forgotten to live.

"Is that an ocean view?" Ren asked now that the picture was really starting to take shape, the lines of blues and greens clearly the ocean.

"Yep."

He'd been in and out of the cabin all day.

They had eaten dinner, which he had prepared—more small game with mixed canned vegetables this time—and she tried to do the cleanup but he'd insisted she spend her time painting. She'd been happy to agree. Now she was back to painting by firelight, like she had last night. Normally that might be frustrating but she didn't care.

"You drawing that from your imagination or from a place you've been?"

She smiled at him over her shoulder. "Believe it or not, this was the view from my back door in Santa Barbara. The Pacific."

"Really? Wow. I can't believe you even pretended to have interest in my family's farm if you had that view to wake up to every day."

She turned back to the painting, laughing. "Well, it wasn't actually my house. I wish I had that sort of money. I'd just been house-sitting for a couple of weeks before I left."

"House-sitting?"

She added another patch of blue that would blend into the gold of the shoreline. "Yeah. Honestly, I don't even know the people who live there. It just fell into my lap. A lady I worked with was supposed to do it but then had to go out of town on an emergency. Next thing I knew I had a close-up view of the Pacific."

Not that she'd taken advantage of it. And

she hoped Olivia didn't get in trouble with the owner since Natalie had left so abruptly.

"Really? You were house-sitting?"

Ren's voice sounded strange. Half-strangled. She turned to look at him. "Yeah. Do they not have a lot of house-sitting in Montana?"

"Not really." He shook his head, looking a little strange. "I guess you were lucky your friend thought of you for the house. What did you guys do together at your job?"

She turned back to the painting. He was fishing for info, as he had been all day. Questions about her childhood, her past, her friends and plans. That should make her nervous, but instead it spread a feeling of warmth through her.

Ren wanted to know more about her.

This sexy, intelligent, insightful man wanted to know more about *her*.

She knew that didn't mean anything, that this…attraction between them couldn't lead to anything permanent, or any sort of serious relationship.

But he wanted to know stuff about her. What harm could there be in telling him about herself? So she had. Not everything, of course, but some. It wouldn't hurt her to tell him about a job she was never going back to.

"Olivia and I worked together at a bar. She

waited tables. I did other stuff. Washed dishes, bussed tables, cleaning."

"Living in California on a dishwasher's salary couldn't be easy, even with house-sitting."

She shook her head without looking away from the door. "You're not kidding. I actually worked two other jobs. Nothing very glamorous, just cleaning office buildings in the mornings. Between the three jobs, I was able to make ends meet." She laughed a little. "Barely."

"Why stay in California at all? It's so expensive there, especially in Santa Barbara."

She shrugged. "Honestly, I was avoiding someone. My ex." There. She'd said it. It hadn't been so hard. "He once said he never wanted to step foot in California ever again. I was sort of hoping that was true."

"How long has it been since you've seen him?"

"Six years."

"He never tried to get in touch with you in all that time?"

No, because he thought she was dead. That was too complicated to even begin telling. "I kept a pretty low profile."

"Sounds like you wanted to stay away from him pretty badly. You had to take some pretty drastic measures."

Oh, God, how had he known that? Had she slipped and said something she shouldn't? She turned slowly. "What do you mean?"

"Even for a farmer who knows what it's like to work seven days a week, working three jobs just to avoid someone is pretty drastic."

If Ren thought that was pretty drastic, telling him how she pretended to be dead would definitely seem like overkill, pardon the pun.

"He was worth avoiding."

She didn't want to talk about Damien. Didn't want to think about him. Out here in this cabin in the middle of nowhere, in this dream where she was doing what she loved to do, with a sexy man watching her and talking to her, Damien had no part.

Ren was already in bed—she'd been so focused she hadn't even realized it—by the time her arms refused to let her do any more work. She was at a good stopping place. Tomorrow she'd finish it.

Then it would be time to get back to the real world. Or at least out of this dream house.

She put away her paints and cleaned her brushes as best she could before turning to her own personal hygiene. She slipped out of her jeans and sweater and into the pajama pants and tank she'd been sleeping in, wishing it was something sexier.

Because she'd already decided that if her time was running out here in the dream cabin, then she wasn't going to waste the time she had left with Ren.

She was going to seduce him, right now.

Chapter Twelve

Of course, wanting to seduce and actually knowing how to seduce were two very different things.

Natalie crawled onto her side of the bed and pulled the covers over herself, staring up at the ceiling without touching him. How come her sleeping body never seemed to have any problem plastering itself all over him, but awake she couldn't even force herself to touch him at all?

Then Ren moved in his sleep, rolled toward her, the shift in the mattress causing her to slide toward him.

Then she just let herself fall the rest of the way into him.

She trailed her fingers across his naked chest, since he just slept in a pair of sweatpants they'd found. She loved touching him, his muscles so defined, yet had never once been used in any sort of violent way against her. The opposite, in fact. Only used to help make her feel secure, safe. Her fingers trailed slightly lower, over his abs. They tensed just the slightest bit under her touch.

"You're awake," she whispered.

"From the second those fingers touched me."

She snatched her hand back. "I'm sorry. You were trying to sleep. I don't know what I'm doing. I—"

She stopped abruptly as he reached out with his own hand and brought hers back down to his chest. "I wasn't complaining about your hand being there."

He slipped his other arm under his head, giving her room to move in a little closer to him. In the soft light of the dying fire he looked so relaxed, half smiling at her with drowsy eyes.

She was never going to get another opportunity like this.

She didn't let herself think about it too much, she just reached in and kissed him. She was tentative, unsure how to show him how she wanted more.

She needn't have worried.

At just the slightest bit of persuasion from her, Ren's mouth was hot and open against hers, his tongue sliding inside, coaxing *her* for more. It was different than the kiss outside

in the snow. Slower, less frantic, more explor-
atory. But no less passionate.

His tongue skimmed across her bottom lip
slowly before nibbling on it, like he had all the
time in the world to taste her and no plans to
ever move from this bed.

Natalie couldn't help it—she sighed into his
mouth, wanting him closer.

Then the kiss changed. Every part of her
hummed with excitement as he pulled her hard
against him, his hand curving around her nape
to hold her there. He moaned against her skin
as his lips worked their way from her ear down
her jaw to her neck.

He grabbed the hem of her shirt like he was
going to pull it over her head—something she
desperately wanted—but then paused.

They were both breathing hard as he leaned
his forehead against hers.

"Natalie...we should stop."

"Oh. This isn't what you want?" She'd been
such an idiot. Just because she'd been attracted
to him and wanted to take advantage of this
time for intimacy didn't mean he did. Maybe
he'd just kissed her so she wouldn't feel bad.
She shot back from him. "I'm so sorry. I—"

"Peaches." His voice was guttural as he
grabbed her and pulled her back against him so
her fingers were once again touching his chest.

"Believe me, I want this. But there's stuff about me you don't know. Important stuff."

He had things he hadn't told her. Logically she already knew that. But they couldn't possibly be as big as the ones she hadn't told him. Her fingers curled into his muscles.

"Is there someone waiting for you at home who will be upset if we do this?"

He gave a shake of his head against the pillow. "No. Nothing like that."

Really, that was all Natalie needed to know. She leaned back in to kiss him, but he stopped her again, holding her by the upper arms while his thumbs drew gentle circles on her shoulders.

"Natalie, you still need to know—"

She cut him off with a finger to his lips. "You know what? There's stuff about me—also important stuff—you don't know. We've both got secrets. But just for tonight, let's leave them out in the snow, okay? For tonight, it's just you and me inside this place. Nothing else. No one else."

His eyes were burning, tortured. "Peaches—"

She brought her lips up to his, replacing her finger, knowing he didn't know how much it was costing her to put herself out there like this, how much his rejection would completely crush her.

"Ren, the only question I need answered right now is whether or not you want me."

He didn't answer her in words. He didn't have to. Instead, his hand gripped the hem of her shirt and pulled it over her head, throwing it to the side. He fisted a handful of her hair as his lips ravished hers, his tongue licking deep into her mouth as if he couldn't get enough of the taste of her.

A hot wave crashed in her chest. She had never felt like this. *Desired* like this. She was drowning in it.

Ren's other hand slid down to her hips, pulling her up against him. Leaving her zero doubt that he did, in very definite fact, want her.

It was amazing and overwhelming. She'd only ever been with Damien and that had never, ever—even at the best of times—felt like this. Like she could gladly stay in this bed for the rest of her life and that would be just fine.

Ren was big and strong and domineering, holding her tight against him as they nestled side by side on the bed, keeping her where he wanted her. But when he rolled over on top of her, covering her with his big body, despite how much she wanted him, wanted this, all her mind could remember was Damien holding her under him. Forcing himself on her even when she didn't want anything to do with him.

She tried to keep kissing Ren, to just push past the ugly memories that tried to creep in, but he noticed.

He sat up, holding his weight on his elbows on either side of her head, using his thumbs to brush her hair off her cheeks. "Hey," he whispered. "What's going on? Did you change your mind?"

She tried to force words out, but they wouldn't come. As tears slid down her temples, he caught them with his fingers.

"Peaches. If you've changed your mind, that's fine."

"I—I got a little overwhelmed." She finally got the words out. "It's been a long time for me. And even before that it…wasn't good."

Anger burned in Ren's eyes but Natalie knew it wasn't directed toward her. Somehow he understood about Damien, had read between the lines, or maybe she hadn't been as secretive as she'd thought when she talked about her past.

Ren rolled his weight off her, and all she could feel was a crushing defeat. All her talk about it just being the two of them inside the cabin and she'd gone and ruined it all. When

Ren sat up she knew he was pulling away and the moment was over.

But instead, he pulled off his sweatpants and lay back down. He put both arms back behind his head, which caused the muscles in his arms and shoulders and chest to ripple.

By the time her eyes made it back to his face he was smiling, his eyes just as smoldering as they'd been a few minutes before.

"Oh," she whispered. "We're not done?"

"Peaches, I've been thinking about you and your soft skin and crystal eyes and haunted smile from the moment I laid eyes on you. Longer, it feels like."

Something dark crossed over his face so fast she couldn't quite decipher it. But whatever it was, he pushed it away and his smile was back.

"Right or wrong, good or bad, smart or stupid, I want you right now more than I've ever wanted any woman. I want to kiss you all over and see if your skin is just as sweet as the peaches and cream my mom used to give me."

She couldn't stop the hitch in her breath. "I want that, too. More than anything. I'm sorry I freaked out."

"No need for apologies. We just need to slow things down. Get it to a speed you're comfortable with." He reached over and grabbed her wrist, giving her a tug so she was once again sprawled on top of his chest. His lips found hers, and all the passion was still there, but with a slow, lush burn this time.

"I've woken up with you like this every morning since I met you. Under you is very quickly becoming my favorite place to be in the world." His thumb brushed along her jawline, sending a rush of sensation skimming across her flesh.

"I thought men wanted to be on top." Damien would've never dreamed of doing anything but dominating her with his body.

Ren's smile was wicked, his hands trailing down her throat, over her chest and breasts, before coming to rest on her waist. "A *real* man wants to be wherever is going to help his woman get what she wants."

"I don't know that I know what I want."

He pulled her more fully on top of him. "Peaches, we've got all night to figure that out."

And they did.

Chapter Thirteen

After their amazing night of lovemaking, trying to tell Natalie the truth hadn't gotten any easier. The entire next day—for the couple hours he let her out of the bed—he'd peppered her with more questions about Freihof, trying to get any info he could.

Justifying to himself that once he told her who he really was she'd likely clam up for good.

She'd opened up more about her marriage and the hell it had been. She'd admitted to running from Freihof, although she hadn't said anything about faking her own death. And finally mentioned that the reason she'd needed to work three jobs was because she was being paid under the table and therefore much less.

Ren had been forced to keep his questions more neutral than he'd wanted.

"You really felt like you couldn't get a regular job? That your ex had the means to find you no matter where you were?"

She glanced away. "Maybe not himself. But Damien has uncanny skills when it comes to getting people to help him. He just has this way of making people believe that he can meet their needs. So I wouldn't doubt for a second that he had someone checking the grid for me every once in a while."

Ren was just beginning to understand the pressure and isolation Natalie had been under for the past six years. He had no doubt she was innocent and that they'd be moving on to the media blitz plan in two more days. The only question now was if she had information locked away inside that could help them.

Before she learned the truth and stopped talking to him altogether.

"What did your ex do for a living?"

She almost seemed to shrink in on herself. "You're going to think I'm an idiot, and I was. All I knew when I got married was that he was a businessman, and had enough money for us to lead very pampered—and isolated—lives. Enough money to pay people to say and do whatever he wanted."

"You never asked later?" Ren realized he probably knew more about Freihof's "business" actions than Natalie ever did. That he'd made his fortune through blackmail, weapon sales and trading of information.

"I learned after he dislocated my shoulder to never ask him anything that might be considered too inquisitive. After he broke my fingers, I learned never to ask any questions at all."

What? Ren walked over to where she was still painting and took the brush from her hands. "He broke your fingers?"

She shrugged, still not looking at him. "It's not a particularly exciting story. He wanted me to be perfect. Was obsessed with me being *perfect*." She all but spat the word. "Whenever I did something that wasn't, there was a punishment. Sometimes my hair wasn't perfectly styled and that garnered a slap."

She began shaking, swallowing hard. "One day after he saw my latest finished painting and disapproved, I asked whether perhaps someone else would like it even though he didn't. He broke every finger on my right hand." She let out a shuddery breath as Ren pulled her into his chest. "I couldn't hold a paintbrush for months. As a matter of fact, I haven't held one since, haven't painted, until now."

He'd lifted her fingers to his lips so he could kiss them. Then took her back to bed. Just to hold her and let her rest, knowing that when she woke up it would be time to tell her the truth. To explain what was really going on and how much they needed her help. Doubly now. One, because she was their best shot, and because of what Homeland Security would do to her when they came barging in here in less than three days.

Hell if Ren was going to allow Natalie to be taken into custody as a hostile informant, suspected of aiding a terrorist. Especially since Ren had been the one to so adamantly argue that to be true three days ago. His judgments about her were what had landed her on Homeland's watch list in the first place.

Now he knew there was absolutely no way. Even if Freihof hadn't done all the terrible things he'd done to her, there was still no way she would assist him. Ren was confident she would be willing to help them make sure Freihof was arrested. Certainly that was in her best interests, but also because it was the right thing to do.

Natalie would need protection after they were out of the wilderness, and not just from Freihof. Obviously someone knew she was alive, or suspected it, based on the deaths of the Baxters. Some enemy of Freihof's, hoping to take her and use her to find him? They'd also put a protective detail on her friend Olivia, just in case someone came after her.

When Natalie woke from her nap, which was plagued by bad dreams, Ren still couldn't find it in him to tell her right away who he was.

Because he knew it would be over. That the sexy, generous woman who'd spent last night and most of today in his arms—hell, even the courageous, friendly woman who'd spent the last two days talking with him—would be gone.

But he had to tell her. He had less than thirty-six hours to get her to understand and ensure her cooperation with the media blitz plan.

He wanted to show her somewhere first. A low overhang that looked out over the river. He could admit it was because he was hoping she would paint it one day.

Not that he'd ever be there to see a finished piece in the future. But he was hoping some part of this place might inspire her to continue painting. Ren and the rest of Omega were going to make sure Freihof never hurt her again.

Broke her damn fingers. No doubt specifically so she couldn't paint, to steal away the obvious joy she derived from it.

That bastard was going down. Ren was willing to pay whatever price it took to make that happen. Had been willing to for a long time.

But he'd never dreamed the price would be the special connection blossoming between him and Natalie. Had never dreamed that would even exist and be so precious to him.

"Ren, where are you taking me?" The exasperation was clear in her voice. He'd made her stop painting, even though she was so close to being finished, and was walking her to the overhang. To share the breathtaking view.

As if that was going to make what he had to tell her—how he'd deceived her—all okay.

"A view. You have to see it for yourself. I think it's right up there with your beach house view."

"You know I don't like snow," she grumbled, but kept walking.

She still hadn't told him why, and he hadn't pushed. He had no doubt it was horrific. "It'll be worth it."

The smile she gave him said she absolutely trusted him to be telling the truth. And his gut clenched even as he wrapped an arm around her and pulled her close.

Beautiful view first, relationship-ending talk after.

He knew the moment she saw it. "Oh, my gosh, Ren!" She hurried up to the edge, looking down over the river just ten feet or so beneath them from here. Most of the edges were frozen but the middle still flowed, giving the entire area a surreal, unearthly look.

"I was hoping you might paint it someday."

She grinned back at him over her shoulder. "Are you kidding? Absolutely. I wish I could paint it right now!"

"I know it's snow, and how much you hate that, but I thought the beauty of it all could trump that."

She spun around to face him. "It does. More than, it…" Her words trailed off as blood drained from her face at something behind him. "Ren, it's a…"

He spun and found a mountain lion just a dozen yards behind them. A huge one. Maybe close to eight or nine feet long. He knew these big cats didn't hibernate and they normally weren't aggressive toward humans. Only under extenuating circumstances like protecting young or…

Then Ren saw it. The animal's slight limp in the back leg as it took a step forward.

He immediately pushed Natalie behind him. "Mountain lion. It's injured or it normally wouldn't be anywhere near us." Ren unzipped his jacket and opened it.

"We need to make ourselves look as big

as possible." He wished like hell he had his Glock. He wouldn't have shot the cat unless he absolutely had to, but even firing above his head would probably scare him off.

Natalie was opening her jacket and standing beside him.

"Peaches, get back behind me."

"No. If being big is what will scare him off, two of us looking as big as possible has to be better."

She was right but he didn't like it. He began yelling loudly and clapping his hands, which also should've scared the animal away. It was definitely not behaving in a normal way. Ren began shifting Natalie slowly toward the side, providing more distance from the cat, yelling the whole time. If they could make it to the set of trees near the edge, Ren could at least use a branch as a weapon if the mountain lion attacked.

When it attacked. If it was going to flee it would've already done so.

He had to turn to use both hands to break off a branch and that was when the giant cat pounced. Natalie let out a terrified scream as he pushed her to the side.

Ren ripped the branch the rest of the way off as the cat landed on him, the force knocking him to the ground. He swung as best he could from the side, but couldn't get much momentum. He felt his jacket and skin rip from the mountain lion's claws.

And then another branch hit it from the side. Natalie, screaming like a banshee, struck the cat as hard as she could. The animal jumped closer to the ledge, dragging Ren with him when its claw got caught in the fabric of his thick coat.

Ren felt the ground beneath him and the cat begin to give way. Natalie was rushing forward to hit the cat again.

"Natalie, no! The ledge is breaking!" Her weight would definitely cause it to fall.

Her eyes were huge as she froze, but it was too late. With a loud crack, the ledge broke away, sending him and the cat into the river ten feet below. The mountain lion jumped away, ripping more of Ren's skin.

Natalie screaming his name from ten feet above was the last thing Ren heard as the icy water of the river sucked him under.

Chapter Fourteen

Natalie screamed Ren's name as he fell from out of her sight and she heard a splash below. She turned and ran as fast as she could to a place where she could slide down to the riverbank, praying the whole time that he was okay and she'd be able to find him.

At the bottom she saw the cat running in the opposite direction, thank God, limping more severely.

"Ren!" she screamed again, looking for him in the sea of white. His head popped up out of the water just a few yards away.

"Oh, my God, Ren!"

Natalie grabbed a branch and skimmed across the edge of the river until she got to a large flat rock that cut into the water, that would put her within just a few feet of him. She wasted no time crawling out on her belly, careful to keep her balance. If she fell in the water, they would both die out here. There'd be no way they'd be able to get back to the cabin.

As she got to the edge she could see Ren's green eyes looking back at her, conscious but in agony as he swam toward her, cold making him sloppy. She threw the branch out to him. He grabbed it as best he could and she pulled him in.

She hooked her arms under his armpits and pulled, using gravity and her own weight to help hoist them backward, and was finally able to drag him out of the water and on top of her. Violent shudders racked his frame and she had to wrap her arms and legs around him to keep him from falling off the rock.

They subsided a little and she got herself out from under him, ignoring the discomfort of her now-wet clothes turning icy. It had to be much worse for Ren.

And if she didn't get him to the cabin and warmed up quickly, his body was going to go into shock. Then shut down.

Reaching under his arms again, she hefted him until they both were on the shoreline.

"Ren!" She rolled him over onto his back and tapped his face with both hands when his eyes began to close. "Come on, solider. I need your help to get you to the cabin."

"Na-Natalie…"

She kissed him hard on the lips. "Yeah, it's me. Now we've got to move before you lose all control of your body." His eyes started to close again. "Ren! I need you to stay awake. We've got to get you on your feet."

Those green eyes looked back at her, glazed with pain.

"I know it hurts," she whispered. Oh, how she knew. "I know everything hurts. Damien used to leave me out in the snow naked, as punishment."

She knew exactly how god-awful the burn was from freezing. Like your whole body had been lit on fire with no chance for relief.

"Ba-bastard."

"He was. Trust me, he was. But I survived and you're going to also. Now I need you to stand."

He nodded jerkily, and she got him to a sitting position. She wrapped one of his icy wet arms around her shoulders, her other arm gripping his waist.

"On three, here we go. One, two, three!"

She used every bit of strength she had, pushing through her legs to get them off the ground. Ren groaned but made it to his feet. She immediately began walking them in the direction of the cabin.

A half mile never seemed so far away.

Ren's face was colorless after just a few steps and she realized he was bleeding from where the mountain lion had mauled him.

They walked slowly but steadily toward the cabin, Ren leaning heavier on her with every step. He wasn't shivering anymore, which she knew was a very bad sign. Natalie was using all the strength she had just to propel them in the correct direction.

"Come on, solider," she said through choppy breaths. "Left. Right. Don't you give up. I'm not leaving you here, so if you stop, we're both going to die. Keep going."

She had to give it to him; he moved one foot in front of the other for a long time. But about halfway there she felt him collapse. It was all she could do to keep him from falling face-first into the snow.

"Ren!" She crouched down and tapped his face lightly again and again but he didn't move. She couldn't even tell if he was breathing. Panicking, she ripped off her gloves and held her fingers to his icy neck, nearly sobbing with relief when she felt his pulse, thready but there.

They weren't far from the cabin but there was no way she'd be able to carry him the last couple hundred yards. They might as well be miles away.

She put her gloves back on and yanked off

her jacket, rolling his torso onto it. Then she grabbed it by the collar and pulled, once again using her weight and gravity to her advantage. Every time she pulled him forward it was by crashing herself into the ground, but at least it moved him.

The progress was slow and agonizing. She had to fall into the snow each time just to get him to move one or two feet. It wasn't long before the cold and exertion was stealing all her strength.

She fought to keep her mind in the present as the agonizing burn of the cold tried to throw her back into the past. When she was helpless. At Damien's mercy.

As the flames of cold licking her skin receded to the blessed numbness, her mind wanted to hide. From the pain, from the exhaustion. To just curl up in the snow and let everything float away.

But if she did, she and Ren would both die. And damn it, she wasn't going to let that happen.

They were less than fifty yards from the cabin—she could see it, for heaven's sake—when her coat ripped under Ren's weight. Sobbing, she stumbled up to the house, grabbed a blanket from the bed and ran back down to Ren.

She laid the blanket out on the ground and used her legs—there was no way she'd be able to do it with her arms—to roll him face-first onto it.

Reaching for an inner strength she didn't know she had, past all the pain of getting them this far, she got them the last few yards and into the house, kicking the door closed behind them. She fell next to Ren on the floor, breaths sawing in and out of her chest.

She just wanted to lie there, but knew she couldn't. They weren't out of the woods yet. Leaving Ren where he lay, she crawled over to the stove. The fire had gone out so she built a new bundle of tinder like he had taught her.

Using the flint with numb, exhausted fingers was even more difficult, but—thanks to Ren and his patience—she knew she could do it. Finally, a spark caught the kindling and a flame began. She built the wood on top of it and opened all the vents on the stove to allow as much heat out as possible.

She pulled off her own clothes, now just as soaked as Ren's, wincing at the pain down the entire back of her body after throwing herself onto the ground time after time to move him. She wrapped herself in a second blanket, crawling back to him. She got his wet clothes off as quickly as her numb, trembling fingers would allow, and wrapped his wound with a T-shirt to stop the bleeding. She threw all the frozen clothes and blanket she'd used to pull him into a pile by the door, just under her painting.

With the last of her strength she grabbed a quilt resting over the back of the couch. She crawled back to Ren where he still lay on the floor, pulled his naked body to hers and wrapped them both as best she could in the blankets. She knew she should try to get him to the bed or closer to the fire, or do more with his wound, but she couldn't. Her strength was gone.

She pulled his icy hands under her armpits and his toes between her calves. She was so cold the difference in temperature barely registered.

She'd done all she could do. She prayed it would be enough.

Blackness claimed her.

EVERY PART OF him was screaming in agony. Ren fought back a moan of pain, years of ops kicking in, not sure where he was and if it was safe to make any sound.

Slowly, awareness came back to him. That damn mountain lion and the icy bitch of a river as it had stolen every bit of breath he had.

But now he was in the cabin with Natalie,

lying on the ground, naked with her in his arms. How the hell had they gotten here?

He shifted, and pain blistered up his shoulder. He moved cautiously, glancing down at the wound. That cat's claws had gotten him good. It was going to need to be stitched.

Natalie rolled, moaning, and her blue eyes blinked open.

"You're awake," she whispered, before her eyes closed again briefly in relief.

Then she frantically sat up and began examining his fingers and toes. "You were wet for so long. I was worried about frostbite but I didn't know what to do and once I got you here I just ran out of steam."

He could feel her poking at his hands and feet as she continued talking. "But they look okay. Thank God." Her hands moved to his shoulder, her voice becoming more and more distressed. "Oh, no, your wound. I knew I needed to do something about it, but I—"

He put his finger to her lips to stop her stream of words, his body burning. "I'm okay. You did great. How did we even get back here?"

"I got you out of the water and you walked part of the way." She shrugged. "Then you lost consciousness and I pulled you the rest of the way on my jacket, then a blanket."

She said it casually as if she hadn't just gone beyond, way beyond, what most people would've been able to do, and saved his life.

He pulled her lips down to his with his good arm. "Thank you. You saved my life."

"I should've done more. I should've—"

"You did enough."

She helped get him up and to the bed. He was barely able to walk, and dizziness assaulted him immediately. Once there, she removed the T-shirt she'd used to stop the flow of blood.

Looking at it, he realized the wound was worse than he'd thought. Skin ripped open and still bleeding. It was already swollen and ugly. Infection was going to be a real worry.

The game was up. He needed to call Omega and get some medical attention out to them. They could have someone here on Jet-Skis within twenty minutes.

Natalie's concerned face was already going in and out of focus. Hell, how was he going to explain this to her?

"I need my phone," he croaked out. She'd covered him with a blanket, but he kicked it off, feeling too hot.

"Ren, we don't get a signal, remember? You've already tried."

He shook his head, the movement causing

him to fall back with a groan. "I have to tell you something. But I need my phone first. Pants pocket."

She moved to the pile of clothes by the door, hanging them over the couch to dry as she came back, but was shaking her head. "I'm sorry, it's broken. The fall in the river and then probably as I dragged you back to the cabin."

When she handed it to him, he realized it was true. There was no way to make a call with this phone. Damn it, they were going to need to walk out of here. As soon as possible.

"You're going to need to stitch this," he told her, struggling to stay upright as everything pitched around him. "There's a first aid kit in one of the kitchen cabinets."

She got it and came back. Ren already knew it was fully stocked, including some supplies for sutures.

She cleaned out the wound, wincing as he bit off a curse at the pain.

"I don't know if I can do this," she whispered as he showed her what she would need to do and helped her prepare the sutures.

"You can." He tried to smile at her but everything was so blurry. He could feel fever beginning to course through his body. "It doesn't have to be perfect. We just need to get it closed before infection sets it."

Although he was pretty sure it already had.

His breath whistled out his teeth as the needle pierced his already inflamed skin. But he swallowed all signs of pain when he saw the tears leaking out of Natalie's eyes.

"You're doing great. You're the most amazing woman I have ever met," he told her after what seemed like hours later when she was almost finished. Her face had long since blurred into an unrecognizable blob as his eyes glazed over from pain. The sound of her voice—the sound of *everything*—starting to seem farther and farther away. He fought every second to stay conscious.

He needed to tell her. Tell her how close they were to civilization. Less than four miles. What if something happened to him and he couldn't lead her out? She could make it. This wasn't just about Freihof anymore.

"Nat, you need to know… I have to tell you…"

"Ren?" Panic was clear in her voice.

And then there was nothing.

Chapter Fifteen

By the time she'd tied off the stitches like he'd shown her how, Ren was completely unconscious.

And burning up with fever.

She touched his forehead but she didn't even have to know for sure how high his temperature had climbed. His face was already a bright red and he'd kicked all the covers off his body. She spent the next few hours alternating between trying to cool him down with a wet washcloth and attempting to get some ibuprofen in him by grinding it into powder and mixing it with water.

Nothing seemed to help.

When the heat in his body turned to chills, she wrapped him in her arms, covered them with a blanket and held him.

"I know you had something you wanted to tell me, so I need you to wake up and try, okay?"

Her voice seemed to soothe his fever-ravaged mind and body so she kept talking.

"You call me Peaches. Did I ever tell you how much I like that? I never would've thought I would, but I really do. It makes me feel...special. Cared for."

His body shuddered again, and she pulled him closer, hooking her leg over his hips to bring him even closer, kissing his forehead.

"I know you've been talking to me and asking me questions. Trying to get to know me. And I know I avoided them a lot."

She knew there was very little chance that Ren was understanding her, but she still wanted to get it all out.

"But I'll tell you, anyway. I married a monster. I was nineteen years old, pretty much alone in the world, and fell for the first guy who showed me attention."

She brushed hair off his forehead.

"You asked me if I knew what he did. I didn't. I really didn't at first. But it didn't take long for me to put it together. He was a criminal. Sold things on the black market. I'm not sure exactly what. Weapons, I think, maybe? Technology.

"I should've gone to the police. The first time I suspected something, or at the least the first time he hurt me. But I had nowhere else to go. He convinced me that nobody would believe me about the abuse."

Talking about this hurt so much.

"But I think maybe he knew I was going to go to the cops, anyway. Before I even knew that was going to be my plan. That's when he changed everything. He fired all the live-in staff who worked at the house, so there was no one around but us.

"Then he told me he was going to train me to be perfect. Teach me how to be the perfect wife. For two and a half years I never saw another living soul but him in that house in Grand Junction. I never stepped foot outside it unless it was some sort of punishment. Like… like the snow. Buried in the snow until I was sure I would die."

She wiped the tears that leaked from her eyes.

"That day it was because I'd forgotten to put the lid back on the toothpaste and clean out the sink. But really that was just an excuse for him to torture me. If it hadn't been that, he would've found something else."

She rubbed her hands up and down Ren's arms. Arms that had never once been used to do anything but bring her pleasure and comfort.

"Eventually I just gave up. Gave in to him.

He wanted the perfect puppet, I realize now. Damien's always been the master puppeteer, getting people to do what he wants. I became an empty shell of a person filled up with the desire to be perfect for him."

Ren stopped shuddering. She almost hoped he could hear her, could process what she was saying, so he would understand. Even though she knew it was probably better for him if he didn't know anything about Damien if the police asked him.

Or, God forbid, Damien coming after Ren himself.

Because telling him this didn't change anything. Didn't change the fact that if Damien discovered she was alive, he would search the world over for her and kill anyone who got in the way of bringing her back to him. Ren included.

"I completely lost myself. Didn't know who I was anymore. Once I was that perfect shell, he could start bringing me places again. A restaurant. The opera. I never talked to anyone, and just sat by his side, the perfect dutiful wife. One day he took me to the bank with him.

"For most people, getting caught in the middle of a bank robbery, getting grazed by a bullet in the head, would be the worst day of their life. For me, it was the best.

"I still couldn't even tell you exactly what happened that day in the bank. Robbers. A SWAT team. Yelling, shooting. I got shot. Well, a bunch of people got shot, but I think my wound actually came from the good guys. Or at least Damien was screaming something like that."

She trailed her fingers along the gauze covering Ren's wound.

"There was blood. So much blood everywhere. Even more than what you lost today. I thought I was dying. Everybody thought I was dying. Damien jumped on a SWAT team member and started hitting him and then got detained, although he didn't get arrested."

If they had arrested and processed him, they would've realized what a criminal they had on their hands. But they'd thought he was just a guy hysterical that his wife had been shot, so they'd let him go.

"Miracle of all miracles, I got brought to the wrong hospital. The closest, but one that was having some sort of biological pathogen scare and was turning away patients. The CDC had been called in and it was complete chaos. I was just sitting in a corner of the ER since everyone had bigger problems than me. I'd stopped bleeding and obviously wasn't going to die. CDC personnel stopped right in front of me, discussing how anyone who had died in the last four hours in the emergency room needed to be immediately cremated because of contamination concerns."

She could swear she almost felt Ren's arms tighten around her. His shuddering had completely stopped. She kicked the blankets off them a little so neither of them would overheat.

"I was sitting there with my own medical file in my lap and knew this was my only chance. Nothing like this was ever going to happen again. I saw the CDC guys tell an orderly to take a woman I was pretty sure was dead, somewhere, and I followed. To make a long story short, I looked at her chart, copied what was said about needing to be cremated. Put my medical file and jewelry in a metal box next to hers and ran."

She rubbed his hair off his forehead again.

"It worked. Everyone assumed I had died in the shootout—I was reported on the news as a victim—and the hospital confirmed they had ordered cremation of all bodies at that time."

She sighed, lying back farther. "That was six years ago. I've been running and hiding ever since. Scared of everything. Haven't even painted. I let him steal so much from me, Ren. Not only the three years I was married to him, but the six years since. Nearly a decade of my life.

"It wasn't until I met you that I realized it was time to stop. Not stop hiding. I'm never going to be able to stop hiding. But stop being his puppet. Stop letting him dictate and control my every move."

She reached over and kissed his forehead, pulling him closer. "You taught me that, Ren. And I love you for it."

IT WAS THIRTY hours before Ren finally woke up. Natalie had bathed him with cool washcloths when he got too hot, held him when he got too cold, fed him as much broth as she could get him to take.

And talked to him through the whole thing.

She realized talking about her life with Damien had been more for her than it had been for Ren, especially since Ren wasn't going to remember any of it anyway. There was so much she'd pushed aside. Feelings of anger, inadequacy, helplessness, pain.

Maybe she was never going to ever truly stop running from Damien physically. But she could stop running every other way.

She was done letting him pull all her strings. Done being a puppet.

Looking at Ren now, watching his body

wake up—his temperature back to normal, the sickly pallor gone, even his shoulder wound looking much better—was like a physical caress.

Natalie knew she hadn't known him long enough to call what was pressing inside her chest legitimate. Knew they were brought on by the dangerous and adrenaline-inducing circumstances that they'd found themselves in. But she didn't care.

She hadn't known she was starving until she'd tasted him.

She wasn't a fool; she knew things would always be complicated at best. But maybe a relationship with him could possibly work. He lived in Montana on a farm, for crying out loud.

A farm that sounded like everything she'd ever wanted in the world.

Why would Damien ever look for her on a farm in Montana? He wouldn't. She could explain everything to Ren, and then stay off the grid there. Take shelter in him. In *them.*

Give in to these feelings that had been wrapping themselves around her heart since the first moment she saw him on the train. And hope he felt the same way.

His green eyes blinked open right then. She

saw confusion light his eyes, then knowledge as he remembered where they were.

Then heat—so much heat—as he focused in on her.

"You're so damn beautiful," he whispered. "From the beginning it has hurt me to look at you."

She felt her face—and other parts of her body—begin to burn.

"I think that might be some residual fever talking there, soldier. You've been pretty sick for a while."

In a heartbeat his face changed, a cool focus washing out the passion that had just crackled between them.

"I've been unconscious?" he asked briskly, already starting to sit up. "How long?"

She moved to help him, but he'd already made it himself. "A few hours."

He pinned her with his eyes, moving his shoulder, testing it. "How many hours? Twelve? Eighteen?"

"Probably closer to thirty. It was sunset two days ago when you fell in. You woke up and helped me stitch you the next morning, and then you were out all day yesterday and a lot of today. It's midafternoon now."

She wasn't expecting the muttered curse that fell from his lips.

She laughed nervously. "Got a big date that you're missing?"

He began patting around the bed. "I need my phone. Do you know where it is?"

"It's broken, remember? You were asking for it before the fever." She got the pieces from the table and brought them over to him. "It got crushed in the fall or the river."

He muttered another curse before standing, completely naked and a little unstable, and walked to the window.

"It's too late. Damn it. I didn't expect this."

Natalie had no idea what he was talking about. "Expect what?"

He didn't answer, just rolled his shoulder and stretched his arm as if to test the usability. It had to have hurt him, but he didn't complain. Then he walked over to the couch where she'd hung his clothes—getting steadier with every step—and got dressed.

"Ren, what's going on?" Obviously she was missing something important. She struggled to keep her voice calm.

He walked to her and cupped her face in his hands. "We have to go. We're going to be walking out this afternoon."

"We are? Why? Where?"

He closed his eyes like he was in pain. More than just the pain in his shoulder. Something deeper. "We're closer to a town than we originally thought. I saw some smoke a few miles away before I fell in the river. So get together whatever you can so we can walk out in about thirty minutes."

"Are you sure we're that close to civilization?"

He walked over to her and leaned his forehead against hers. "Yes. I'm positive. I just wanted a little more time with you alone before giving you back to the rest of the world. And then the mountain lion…"

He still looked pained. She knew he wasn't telling her everything. But what he was telling her was enough.

She smiled and kissed him softly. "I don't think I wanted to go back to the rest of the world, anyway. Go do whatever it is you need to do. I'll be ready in thirty minutes. I trust you."

Chapter Sixteen

I trust you.

The words echoed through Ren's mind as he stepped outside the cabin and moved quickly through the trees where he kept the lock-box with items he thought he might need: his Glock, Omega badge, a set of handcuffs.

Another phone right now would be pretty damn handy, too. Although it would be too late to call off the agents Homeland Security had sent.

He'd run out of time while he was unconscious. He knew they were here to take Natalie. To confine her in a windowless box of a room and force her to tell them every single detail about her life with Damien Freihof.

He remembered parts of what she'd said to him while he'd be in and out of delirium with fever.

I married a monster.
Buried in the snow.

Perfect shell.

I love you.

He slammed the bottom of his fist against the tree, gritting his teeth at the reverberations that coursed through his arm and wounded shoulder. It was no less than he deserved.

Natalie was completely innocent. She was good and gentle and kind. Brandon and Andrea had tried to warn Ren of that from their first meeting with her, but he hadn't wanted to believe it.

And now Homeland Security wanted to take her in and break her. Not through physical torture, but they wouldn't need to use that. Because there were so many ways someone as gentle as Natalie could be broken.

Like learning she'd given her heart to and trusted the wrong person.

He clamped down on the howl that wanted to rip from his throat. Because at the end of it all, it wouldn't be Homeland Security's brutish methods that would break Natalie.

It would be Ren's attention and kindness.

But hell if he was going to let them take her. She might be heartbroken by the time this was all done, but he wasn't going to let her mind and spirit be crushed by what they would do to her. And he knew agents were out here right now, preparing to seize the cabin and take Natalie in.

He stayed low, moving outward toward the higher ground that would give him the tactical advantage. If he had to guess, there were probably two or three agents out here for the arrest. Two who would knock openly on the door—especially since they thought they had another law enforcement officer inside who would help with the arrest—and a third who would stay hidden and make sure there were no surprises.

Ren would take out that third agent first.

From up on the ridge he could see the snowmobiles they'd used to get here, leaving them parked half a mile away to keep sound from traveling to the cabin. He would need to work quickly to disarm the first guy before the other two burst through the cabin door. And do it all without killing or seriously injuring the other law enforcement officers.

He spotted them—three just like he'd thought—as they were splitting off from one another. All three already had their sidearms out, which meant they were definitely taking this seriously.

Ren moved quickly in the direction the backup man had gone. He estimated he had about five minutes to disarm and subdue this one before the other two entered the cabin.

Ignoring the pain from his injuries and weakness from a day and a half ravaged by fever, Ren moved silently between the trees. He kept his own sidearm holstered at his waist. No matter what, this couldn't become a shoot-out.

Ren knew these woods much better than the agents, and they weren't expecting anyone to be out among the trees. Agent Three was looking in the direction of the cabin when Ren moved up behind him, got out his weapon and knocked him on the back of the neck.

The man crumpled to the ground without a sound. Taking out his handcuffs, Ren bound the man around a small tree, then used a ripped part of his shirt as a gag. He hadn't hit him that hard; the guy was already groaning and would be awake in a couple of minutes.

"Be back with your friends in just a second, buddy," Ren whispered, then ran toward the other two agents.

One had just peeked through the window to see what was happening inside the cabin, and was signaling to the other. Ren needed to get them far enough away that there wouldn't be any chances of Natalie hearing them.

"Hey, fellas," he called softly from behind

them, Omega ID already in hand, praying this would work.

They swung around with weapons raised but he'd been expecting that. Ren kept his credentials out toward them, while raising a finger to his lips.

"Ren McClement, Omega Sector. Been waiting for you guys to get here for a while."

They lowered their weapons exactly like he'd wanted them to do.

"McClement, what are you doing out here rather than in there with the suspect?" Agent One asked.

Suspect, not witness. Not informant. That confirmed everything he needed to know.

"We were told that Omega didn't necessarily want us butting in," the second man said, the look they gave each other clearly stating they didn't care what Omega Sector wanted. The two law enforcement organizations were independent of each other, neither under the other's jurisdiction. Generally, they were after the same bad guys and it rarely caused conflicts.

Today there would definitely be conflict.

Ren motioned them closer to him, farther from the cabin, and they came. When they got close enough, he stuck out his hand like he wanted to shake. "Like I said, I'm Ren."

"Mark Jaspers," the first guy said. "And this is—"

Ren didn't wait for the second introduction. He grabbed Jaspers's outstretched arm and yanked, pulling him forward and into a vicious punch to the jaw that knocked him to the ground.

Not-Jaspers witnessed it, and was in the process of pulling his weapon back out when Ren swung around and roundhouse kicked him, knocking the gun into the trees. An uppercut to the jaw had the other agent stunned and stumbling backward.

"What the hell?" Jaspers croaked from the ground as Ren grabbed not-Jaspers by the collar and threw him down next to Jaspers, pointing his Glock at both men. "What the hell are you doing, McClement?"

"Sorry, guys, but I'm not going to be able to let you take Ms. Anderson today." There was no damn way he was calling her Mrs. Freihof.

"Are you in on it with her?" not-Jaspers asked. "Working with Freihof?"

"No," Ren spat. "But neither is she. And she doesn't know where he is. She's running from him."

Jaspers tried reason. "Why don't you just let us take her in, make that clarification for ourselves? I'm sure if you've found it to be true, we will, too."

"No offense, guys, but I've seen the tactics you use when questioning someone you consider to be hostile." Never quite enough food, water, sleep. No bed. Sitting in hard chairs in windowless rooms for hours upon hours. Ren had never felt bad about it when it was someone who knew something that law enforcement needed to know in order to save lives.

But it damn well wasn't happening to Natalie.

"Omega has a plan in place to draw Freihof out," Ren continued.

"You missed that deadline this afternoon, McClement," Jaspers said. "You didn't report in, didn't show up. You missed your chance."

"There were circumstances that couldn't be helped. The plan will still work. So I'm just going to keep you guys here a few extra hours until I can get her out and in front of the media. Freihof will come." Ren knew that for an absolute fact now that he knew what had happened between them. How Freihof had tried to control every part of her life. Letting Natalie wander free without him wouldn't even be an option.

"You do this, your career is over," not-Jaspers said. "It won't matter if it's for the greater good or not. Your time with Omega will be done."

Ren already knew that. Had known it as soon as he'd come up with this plan. But he didn't grieve the choice. It was time to stop living in the darkness that had been his constant companion for so long. Step into the light.

Natalie and her innate generosity of spirit and kindness had shown him that in such a very short time. He prayed there would be some way to get her to forgive him for what he'd done, what he was about to do. Some way to get her to share the light with him, once they had taken Freihof out for good and he could never hurt her again.

He brought Jaspers and his partner into the woodshed and tied them, before going back to get Agent Three—now conscious—and brought him back also.

"There will be someone here to release you guys in the next couple of hours. Just don't get yourselves killed in the meantime."

"You're done, McClement," Jaspers bit out. "Your entire career washed down the drain. I hope she's worth it."

Ren moved a gag over the other man's mouth. "She is."

Ren took a phone from one of the agents and stepped outside, immediately calling Omega.

"Steve Drackett."

"I'm going to need a Homeland Security cleanup in aisle four."

"Damn it, Ren. You missed the deadline. What the hell is going on? I was about to send agents in there myself. What happened?"

"It's a long story involving a mountain lion and near death."

Steve actually chuckled. "Doesn't it always?"

"Are we too late for the media blitz?"

"I can maybe keep the press here in Riverton for thirty more minutes." Steve's voice was tight. "They passed restless two hours ago."

Ren grimaced. They would need to take a snowmobile. He would move the other out of her path and tell her he ran into some hunters. But this meant more lies to Natalie and not enough time to explain about the whole plan.

Who Ren was. What he needed her to do. She'd be blindsided.

But there was no other way. He had to get her in front of the cameras. Once that happened, Homeland wouldn't take her out of play if she was the best bet of luring Freihof in.

"Do it. We're on our way. We'll be there in twenty-five."

"Please God, tell me there are no dead Homeland Security agents at that cabin."

"No, but some very pissed-off ones. You need to send someone to get them in the woodshed."

"You know those guys can make your life hell, right? We may not work for them, but they have the ear of pretty powerful people."

Ren took a calming breath. "I know. I crossed a line. I'm done."

The other man said nothing for a long second, then ironically echoed Jaspers's words. "I hope she's worth it, my friend."

His answer was still the same.

"She is."

Chapter Seventeen

Like she promised, Natalie had all their stuff returned to the backpacks, and had even cleaned up as best she could, when Ren arrived back a little over thirty minutes later.

He strode through the door and walked right up to her, lifting her in a one-armed hug with his uninjured limb.

"What?" she said as he kissed her, ignoring the pain from her hurt back. There was a desperation to him she'd never seen before.

"We have to leave right now."

"Oh." She'd known that was coming but had hoped he would come back and say they had more time. She liked it here. Just the two of them and her painting.

He closed his eyes for a moment, almost like he was fortifying himself before reopening them. "I ran into some hunters. They gave me a snowmobile to use to get us into town. But we've got to go right now. My family got word of the accident and they've been frantic. I need to get in touch with them right away."

She felt terrible. Of course they needed to go. "Sure. I'm ready."

"Peaches. I…" He stepped away from her, eyes tortured. "When we get there, everything will change."

"I know." She'd always known that. "The real world. It's okay."

He looked at the phone in his hand. "Damn it, we've got to go right now." He rushed over to the door and ushered her out. "Just, once we get to Westwater, stay near me, okay? I promise I will explain everything as soon as I can."

Westwater? That was the nearby town? Natalie forced herself to breathe down the panic. She'd known they were somewhere in or near Colorado, but had no idea they were so close to Grand Junction where she'd lived with Damien.

It didn't matter. She would get out of here as soon as she could. Maybe she wouldn't be able to go to Montana with Ren right away, but she could meet him there later. There was so much they needed to talk about.

Ren got her situated on the snowmobile, before sitting behind her, surrounding her with his warmth.

"We'll need to talk," he said. "I ran out of

time, and that's on me, but just promise me we'll talk when we get there. That you'll give me a chance."

She turned to look at him over her shoulder and smiled. "Of course." There was nothing she wanted more.

He didn't smile back, that tortured look still in his eyes as he put the only helmet over her head, started the machine and soon had them flying.

The faster they sped, the more worried Natalie became. Something must be pretty desperately wrong for him to move them at such a reckless pace.

Less than twenty minutes later he stopped them. She could see the lights of the town a few hundred yards away, but he didn't drive the snowmobile all the way in, even though it probably wouldn't even be that uncommon.

He stood and helped her take off her helmet.

"Why did we stop? A lot of Colorado towns allow the use of snowmobiles on the street."

He began walking, holding her hand. "We have to walk the rest of the way and there are things you need to know before we make it into town."

Her gut tightened, but she kept up her steps with him. "Okay."

"Natalie, I haven't been completely honest with you."

"About what?" She almost stumbled over a root sticking up on the uneven ground but he held on to her arm, righting her.

He grimaced, continuing to propel them forward. "About a lot. I need your help. It's important. Bigger than you or me. Or even us. A lot of lives are at stake."

"Ren, what's going on?" she whispered.

He stopped and ran his hand through his brown hair. They were just on the outskirts of town. "God, Peaches… Natalie… I never meant…"

"McClement!" A woman rushed into the woods. "Thank God. You guys have got to move right now. We're going to miss our window to hit the evening news if you don't."

Natalie just watched as Ren turned to the woman, not correcting her at the wrong name.

"Lillian, I need a few minutes. Natalie doesn't know what's going on."

He knew this woman?

And what was it that Natalie did not know? Evidently a lot.

Lillian just shook her head. "What the hell have you been doing in that cabin for the last five days if not explaining what we need?"

She looked back and forth between Ren and Natalie. "Oh."

The petite woman who sounded vaguely familiar turned to glare at Ren as she obviously figured something out. Something Natalie still couldn't. "Damn you, McClement. But we're still out of time. We've got to go."

As she came closer, Natalie realized this was the same woman who had sold her the ticket for the train. Why would she even be here?

Natalie grabbed the woman's arm gently. "Why are you here if you work for the bus company?" Maybe the train and bus company were owned by the same corporation or something.

The compassion—*pity*—in the other woman's eyes made Natalie's heart sink more.

"You just need to come with us," Lillian said, taking another moment to glare at Ren. "Don't say anything, okay? Just let Ren do the talking."

"Do the talking to who?"

Neither Lillian nor Ren answered. Lillian just wrapped an arm around Natalie's waist and led her toward the town.

Just before they made it onto the streets, Lillian grabbed a walkie-talkie from her waist and spoke into it. "Sheriff, I found them! They're here on the west side of town near Mill Road!

Going to need medical, but they're both alive and relatively unharmed!"

The excitement in her voice was in direct opposition to the anger in her eyes for Ren.

"Damn it, I told everyone to use the private channel if we learned anything." The sheriff came back on the walkie-talkie a moment later. "The press is on this channel."

"Oopsies," Lillian said. "Sorry, Sheriff. I forgot."

She most definitely had not forgotten.

"I don't understand what's happening," Natalie whispered. Every second her heart sank lower in her chest.

"Congratulations. You and Ren are hikers who have been lost for nearly a week and have somehow miraculously survived."

Natalie shook her head. "But we weren't hiking. We were on the train. The train you sold me a ticket to."

"Natalie…" Ren reached for her, but she took a step back.

She could see people rushing toward them now. A lot of people. People with lights and cameras.

"What have you done?" she whispered. Not wanting to believe what she was finally beginning to understand. Ren had been using her.

"I've got to go," Lillian said. "I can't be in any of the press footage. Freihof knows me."

Lillian knew Damien.

Ren knew Damien.

Natalie fought to hold on as the whole world spun around her, the snow seeming to rise up and swallow her whole. She couldn't fall. Couldn't allow it to bury her.

Because this time no amount of begging was going to get her out.

THE NEXT HOUR passed in a blur for Natalie. Just before the press had completely descended on them, Ren had ripped his jacket open just a little farther so his wound was more noticeable.

They'd been led to the high school auditorium, quickly checked out by a medic, then sent in front of the cameras. Ren kept Natalie plastered to his side. When it became obvious she wasn't interested in—or capable of—much response, the reporters had turned all their questions to Ren.

He answered them with practiced ease.

They were two hikers whose GPS had failed and then they had gotten caught in a freak storm. No mention of a train crash at all. When Natalie glanced over to the side and saw the young man with the sandwich who had hit on her on the train, still very much alive, she realized the extent of what was going on.

It had all been a setup. From the very beginning. The moment she'd set foot in the bus station. She couldn't even fathom the resources it had taken to fool her to such a degree.

Ren answered more questions as Natalie glanced the other way and saw Brandon and Andrea, the Omega Sector agents who'd come to her house, standing in a darkened corner. Andrea smiled gently at Natalie, an obvious attempt at some sort of apology for what was happening, but Natalie just ignored it. They were all working together. Every single event and action of the past week had been in careful deliberation to get them right here in front of dozens of news cameras.

Where Damien would be sure to see her.

Ren, or Warren Thompson, as he'd been introduced, was great with the reporters. Charming. Handsome. So photogenic that every producer in the country probably couldn't wait to get this happy-ending story in front of as many viewers as possible. Ratings through the roof.

"A mountain lion, not behaving normally because it had been injured, became aggressive and attacked me. If it hadn't been for Natalie…"

The reporters launched into more questions that he answered.

"Natalie pulled me out of the river.

"Natalie amazingly managed to get my unconscious half-frozen carcass to the hunter's cabin.

"Natalie was able to stitch me up.

"Natalie is very definitely the reason I'm still alive and we're both here."

She realized he was saying her name over and over for a reason: to draw attention to it. So that any soundbites that were used had a better chance of including her name.

"Natalie and I are truly touched by the onslaught of support and thankful to be alive. But I'm sure you can appreciate how tired we are and our need to be more thoroughly checked out by medical professionals, but we will definitely be here for at least three or four more days, until we're cleared to travel. On behalf of both Natalie and me, thank you."

Her name again. They were throwing her in Damien's face.

She was bait.

And she had no doubt at all that Ren had just signed her death warrant.

Chapter Eighteen

Natalie was alive.

After talking to the people who'd owned the Santa Barbara house had proved to be a dead end, Damien had been forced to wait, wondering if it was all true. Until he could see her with his own eyes, he wouldn't be able to believe it.

Waiting for another call to come in concerning her on the tapped phone had been agonizing. And even when it had come, the information hadn't quite made sense. But it had gotten him the information he needed: something was happening in Riverton and it concerned Natalie.

He'd had to keep a very low profile since this tiny little town had been crawling with Omega agents for the last day and a half. He'd seen Brandon and Andrea Han, not to mention SWAT team members Lillian Muir and Ashton Fitzgerald. All people he'd battled in the past.

It would've been so easy to take them out one by one. But that would've cost him his chance to see Natalie. To see if it was really Natalie they were so convinced was alive.

He had no doubts now.

He could feel rage crashing through his system. It was all he could do to remain behind the large video camera in the high school auditorium, careful to keep his face hidden, rather than run up onto the stage, grab her and escape.

Natalie was alive.

Not only that, she was fully aware of who she was and what she was doing. Which meant only one thing: she had deliberately run from him six years ago. Deceived him.

Defied him.

His fingers clenched around the edge of the camera until he felt pieces of plastic break off in his hands. He forced himself to breathe in and out deeply, to get his rage under control.

There would be plenty of time to correct Natalie's behavior. To punish her. To teach her that her conduct was unacceptable.

He looked at her tucked up against the man who was speaking. This Warren Thompson fellow who seemed to have the press eating out of his hand. Was he a member of Omega Sector? Damien didn't know, had never seen him or heard his name, although he'd spent extensive time studying the organization.

It didn't matter. He would have to die, of course. He dared to touch the perfect Natalie? The man must die.

Sadly, it was probably time for Natalie to die, as well. If she was willing to deceive Damien in this way, to throw away their perfect marriage, then she obviously was broken beyond repair.

Maybe with enough correction, enough punishment, she could be fixed. Probably not, but he wouldn't know until he tried.

Omega Sector once again was putting themselves between Damien and what belonged to him. And Natalie did belong to him whether she wanted to accept it or not.

No matter. Omega would soon be so busy trying to clean up the mess he'd made with his handy-dandy biological canisters that Natalie would be the last of their worries.

Couldn't she feel it? The pull between them? The connection even from across the room? Not once did she even look up, so he had to assume she'd lost touch with what had been so special between them.

It was a shame Natalie would have to die, but it couldn't be helped. As a matter of fact, his lovely wife had just helped him make the decision about where to release the biological contaminants.

His perfect wife was gone. He would punish her, then bury her.

And this time when she died, she would truly be dead.

Chapter Nineteen

An hour later Ren was calling himself every foul name he could think of. He'd expected Natalie's anger. For her to fume, scream, throw a few punches at him.

He would've gladly taken them over her blankness.

He hadn't been making it up when he'd told the press they'd needed a thorough examination by the medics. The doctor had winced at the ugly sight of the stitches in his shoulder, but had declared that they would do the job. It would just mean that Ren would always have a scar there, much more pronounced than it would've been if he'd been stitched by a professional in the hospital.

Ren had a feeling he was going to have much more than just this one scar by the time this mission was over.

The doctor had given him an antibiotic shot to help fight off any remaining infection and declared him in fairly good health, all things considered.

Ren had demanded to see Natalie immediately. He needed to talk to her. To explain.

As if she hadn't figured it out already by herself.

Panic had him entering the room where she was being examined immediately after knocking. Like him, Natalie had been given a new set of clothes. She was facing the opposite direction, pulling a sweater down over her back.

A back covered in bruises.

"What the hell is wrong with your back?" he growled.

Natalie pulled the sweater the rest of the way down, spinning toward him.

"I realize you're in charge of this operation, Agent McClement," the Omega medic said. "But please wait for permission to enter an examination room in the future."

Ren ignored the doctor. "What's wrong with your back?" he asked Natalie.

Her eyes just stared at him. No anger. Just blankness. Totally withdrawn. She sat down in a chair and began putting on tennis shoes that had been provided for her.

She obviously wasn't going to answer so he turned to the medic. "What happened?"

He didn't look like he was going to answer,

either, so Ren took a quiet step forward. "You can either tell me now, or I can read your report in an hour, which will be your last here before you start looking for a new job. If she's injured I need to know about it for this operation."

And because how the hell had he not known she was hurt?

"Ms. Anderson has extensive bruising on her back, shoulders and hips from repeated contact with the ground. Painful, but nothing that won't heal in the next few days."

Ren turned to Natalie. "How did you come in constant contact with the ground enough to bruise that much?"

She didn't answer, just kept messing with her shoelaces like they contained the answer to every mystery in the universe, although she still hadn't tied them.

He turned back to the medic.

"Evidently it took concerted effort to get you from the frozen river, back to the cabin. Ms. Anderson didn't have the strength to get you there on her own, so she used momentum and gravity to move you forward. Unfortunately that meant throwing herself onto the ground over and over. So…extensive bruising."

Ren ran a hand over his face. "Thank you."

He moved to crouch down in front of Natalie, who was still messing with her shoelaces. Gently brushing her fingers aside, he tied her shoes for her, then placed his hands on her ankles until she finally looked at him.

What rested behind those blue eyes was just as bruised as her back and hips, if not more so. He had known it wouldn't be easy to explain what he'd done, why they needed her help to catch her ex.

But he never dreamed it would put this look in her eyes. Haunted. Empty.

Bruised.

"Peaches…"

She shook her head. "No." Her voice was hoarse as if she'd screamed until it had broken. "Don't you dare call me that."

Ren turned back to look at the medic. "Are you done here? Can she and I talk alone?"

The man nodded and walked out. Ren stepped back and leaned against the table.

"I work for—"

"Omega Sector. Yeah, I figured that part out already."

"How?"

She looked at him before turning to study the wall. "I saw that couple, Brandon and Andrea, who were at the Santa Barbara house last week, during the press conference. I saw the guy who hit on me on the train there, too, so I'm assuming it was all a setup. No real train accident."

He nodded. "Yes, that's correct."

"I suppose I should be glad nobody died. Although I've been so caught up getting laid that it wasn't like I really cared, anyway."

Ren gripped the table forcefully. "Don't you dare talk about yourself—what we shared—that way. You thought you were *surviving*. There was no shame in what you did or how you reacted."

"I'm sure you see it that way," she whispered, looking away.

"I mean it. You want to be mad at me for what I did, how I deceived you, that's fine. You have every right. But you did nothing wrong."

He wished she would get mad at him. Anything would be better than this blankness. A shell of the woman he knew.

I completely lost myself. I was the perfect shell.

Tendrils of memories flowed through his mind. Words she'd said while he was in and out of the fever.

"Natalie, Omega Sector is a powerful law enforcement agency. The best of the very best. We're going to protect you."

She just shook her head.

"Three weeks ago your ex-husband was part

of a plan that would've killed tens of thousands of people if Omega hadn't stopped him. Freihof has also been responsible for the killing or wounding of multiple agents and civilians over the last few months. When we discovered you were alive we thought we might be able to obtain a clue about his whereabouts."

Now she looked at him. "I don't know where he is. I've spent the last six years hiding from him in case he figured out I was alive."

"I know that now, but I didn't at the time. You were staying in a million-dollar beach house, going to work in fancy office buildings each day. It looked like maybe you were either working with Freihof or providing for him in some way."

"I wasn't," she whispered.

"I know," Ren repeated. He could feel his heart ripping in two. "And we were going to follow you, talk to you, see what happened and how you might possibly help us catch him. Then we discovered that Damien had obtained biological weapons. We were out of time. We needed to use any and all means necessary to find him."

"Including this elaborate plan involving me."

"Especially you. He's always been obsessed with you. His attacks on Omega Sector, killing agents and their loved ones, were in direct retaliation for what he thought Omega SWAT did to you at that bank six years ago. They were the ones who came in to fight against the robbers."

Her fingers covered her eyes. "That SWAT team saved my life by nicking me in the head. I have no doubt I'd be dead right now at Damien's hand if not for what happened."

It was time to tell her everything.

"Andrea and Brandon came to see you, to ascertain if you knew anything, or if you'd be willing to help. They still weren't sure if you had ties to your ex when they left. But mostly we put them in play to get you to run. To shake you up."

She laughed, the sound hollow. "You certainly did that."

"We set up the crash to see if you would call Freihof when there was an emergency. When you were sure there wasn't anybody following."

"Except you."

He nodded. "Except me. I was hoping I'd come across as a nice enough guy that you wouldn't worry that I was law enforcement."

"That I would accept that you were just a Montana sheep farmer." She laughed again, hysteria lacing the sound. "God, I'm the biggest idiot on the planet."

Ren crouched down at her feet again. "No. My parents do have a sheep farm in Montana. I don't work there, but—"

"Is your name even Ren?"

"Ren McClement. Just Ren, not Warren. Although many people assume it's a shortened name. Thompson is my mother's maiden name." He touched her ankles again, then let them go when she flinched. "It didn't take me long to figure out that you had nothing to do with Freihof or his actions."

"And once you did that? Then what was your grand plan?"

He strung his fingers through his hair. "First, I wanted to make sure you didn't know anything—details—subconsciously. So I just tried to talk to you."

"While I was painting."

"Yes. Then—I swear, Natalie—I was taking you out to show you that river so you could see something beautiful, a place I would always remember and wanted you to remember, too. Wanted you to paint, before I told you what we needed you to do back here with the press. But then that damned mountain lion and the fever…"

"You should've told me, Ren," she whispered. "Once you woke up. You should've told me."

"I know. I wanted to. But we were out of time. I had been unconscious much longer than I'd thought. Homeland Security was sending agents out to detain you as a hostile subject. They would've thrown you in a cell."

"But I have nothing to do with Damien!"

"It wouldn't have mattered, not to them—they would've detained you indefinitely. There were three agents already at the cabin when we left. They should be getting rescued from the woodshed where I tied them up right about now. I couldn't let them take you. And then I had to get you here in front of the cameras so they couldn't arrest you, because now the plan is already in play."

She just shook her head and looked over to the side. Ren stayed where he was, crouched down in front of her, unable to bear to put distance between them, afraid they'd never be close again.

Not that he could blame her.

"I would've told you, Natalie. I promise. I just ran out of time. We needed your help. Freihof has to be stopped before he can use those biological weapons."

"And the lovemaking? Where did that fall in your great scheme? Since it seems like you planned everything down to the letter."

The time for lies was over. "It was always a

possibility if that would help me get closer to you, to get you to contact Freihof. He's going to kill thousands of people if we don't stop him. I was willing to do just about anything, including faking intimacy with the woman I thought might be in league with him."

He moved slightly closer to her, not expecting her to respond. "But it didn't take me long to figure out you weren't working with him. The opposite—you were running from him. It didn't take me long to see the brave, kind, smart woman you were. I made love to you purely for selfish reasons. Because I couldn't stay away from you. I had to know how you felt, how you tasted."

He touched her ankles—hell, he would stay here perched at her feet forever if it meant she would listen to him, forgive him, give them another chance—his heart swelling when she didn't flinch away again.

"I did everything wrong with this case, Peaches. Everything I told you, all the stories, facts about my life, almost every single part of it was true. I wanted to get to know you, and I wanted you to know the real me."

"Family farm?"

"True."

"Special forces?"

He nodded. "Also true. These are all things

I never should've been honest about in an undercover operation. If you'd been playing me, you would've known things about me—about my family—that could destroy me and them. But I couldn't stop myself from telling you. Just like I couldn't stop myself from asking about all of you. Not just the stuff that might possibly help us catch Freihof."

"So plan B or Q, or whatever derivative you ended up at, was to ask me to out myself. To give up the tiniest bit of safety I've had for six years and rub the fact that I'm alive in his face. To be bait."

"We will protect you. He won't get anywhere near you. We just needed to get him to show up where we are ready, for him to go on the defensive." He moved closer. "I would've asked you, Peaches. Begged you to help, if needed. Explained about the biological weapons and how many people he could kill indiscriminately."

"I already knew Damien was a monster. Did I ever tell you about how one of his favorite games when I didn't do something right, didn't do something perfect, was to choke me until I stopped breathing and then revive me? Or leave me trapped in a cage while he left the house? Sometimes for days?"

She moved her legs away from his touch,

but her voice held no emotion as she said the words. No anger. No fear. She should be screaming, railing, not sitting there in the chair like she was discussing the weather.

She was in shock. He needed to give her more time to adjust to what he was, who he was, what had happened. It was unreasonable to expect her to just be okay with it.

In many ways he wished she was furious at him, even hated him, screaming that she would never forgive him. That would be better than this despondency.

He put his hands on the outside of her chair, trapping her in his arms in the only way he knew how. "I'm sorry, Peaches. Sorry that I didn't think there was any other way to do this. Sorry that you were too damn gorgeous and delicious for me to resist in that cabin, even though it broke every rule I've ever had. Sorry that I blindsided you with the press when we got here. But I knew, deep in my gut, that you would help us. That you would play the role you needed to in order to help us draw Freihof out. To save so many lives."

She stared at him with those bruised blue eyes for long moments. "Yes, you're right. I've always been the perfect puppet."

"Natalie…"

She stood, and he stood with her. He wanted

to pull her into his arms, to just hold her. Not that it would make everything okay or even bring her closer to forgiving him, but because she looked like she was about to crack into a million pieces.

"No." She held a hand out, stopping him. "You can't touch me. Not right now. I'm sorry."

"Don't be sorry. I understand."

She gave a self-deprecating shake of her head. "You're right. I shouldn't be sorry." She walked toward the door, turning back as she reached it.

"You were right, Ren. Your gut was right. I would've helped you draw Damien out. Maybe not at first, like when Brandon and Andrea came to talk to me. But once I understood the true scope of the situation, I would've helped."

"I know," he whispered, feeling his heart crack a little more in his chest.

"You're a good man who had a job to do that I happened to be part of. I know that. You had to do what you had to do. Me included."

He couldn't help it—he was at her side of the room in seconds, arms trapping her once again as he brought his forehead to the side of her head. Breathed in her scent.

"Nothing about us was fake, Natalie. Not being able to keep my hands off you was the truest thing I've ever felt. I regret that I wasn't able to be honest with you, but I'll never regret the days we spent together in that cabin. Getting to know you. Getting to taste you. Getting to love you."

He felt her suck in a shuddery breath, leaning into him just the slightest bit.

"Then I'll tell you what I would've told you if we'd come at this problem together from the beginning. If I'd been working with you and had agreed to all this."

"What?"

"I won't blame you for what happens. And you shouldn't blame yourself."

"What do you mean?"

"When Damien finds me and takes me…" Her voice cracked. "Whatever it is he ends up doing to me, it's not your fault."

His teeth ground in his jaw. "Not. Going. To. Happen."

Now she turned completely to him, stepped closer and rested her forehead on his chest.

"You trust your gut. It's what makes you a good agent. Made you a good solider. Your gut told you this plan was going to work and I was going to help you."

He kept his arms braced on the wall even though her head was touching his chest. He knew she didn't want to be pulled to him. "Yes. I trust my gut."

"I trust my gut, too. And my gut says that Damien is going to find me and he's going to kill me."

Chapter Twenty

"By now Freihof will have seen the footage of Natalie. Our best estimates based on where he was last seen in South Carolina are that he will be here in twenty-four to thirty hours," Brandon Han said. A big chunk of the Omega Critical Response team—including Brandon's wife, Andrea, Steve Drackett, Lillian Muir and Aston Fitzgerald—were all sitting around the kitchen table of the safe house on the outskirts of Westwater.

These were the people who had faced down Freihof in the past, who had, or very nearly had, lost everything to him. The ones who were most invested in catching him.

"So we give him twelve hours tops before we're on red alert," Fitzgerald shot back. "Because we all know that Freihof is always at least one step ahead of where we think he is."

Ren was listening to the team but his eyes were on Natalie. He'd tried to talk her into sleeping. Even had Andrea try. Natalie had rested for about twenty minutes, but had been up wandering around the house for the last half hour.

"We have law enforcement at every major airport looking for him. Hopefully he is so desperate to get to her quickly that he'll decide air travel is worth the risk," Steve said. "We've also got all smaller regional airports on alert. If anyone files a sudden flight plan to any of the airports within a hundred and fifty miles of here, we'll get a notification. But our guess is he'll probably drive, rather than risk detection."

"I'll still be ready with my sniper rifle by dawn," Ashton, one of the best marksmen in the country, assured them. Freihof had dared to bring Ashton's beautiful toddler daughter into this bloody fight, a fact Ashton wouldn't be forgetting any time before ever.

Natalie walked to another window, looking out it, her arms wrapped protectively around her middle. No amount of words had been able to convince her that they weren't going to let Freihof get to her.

Brandon looked in Natalie's direction also. "We'll do one more press interview with Natalie in the morning. Just to make doubly sure she's seen, then we'll get her to Omega HQ for safety."

She had to be able to hear them, but nothing changed about her demeanor to indicate that she was listening at all. She just walked over to the door and stood looking at it. Then began to gently rock herself back and forth, just like she had…

Damn. Ren was out of his chair and over to her in an instant, her face confirming what he'd feared. She hadn't been just wandering around the house. She was panicking over the door and window locks like she had in the cabin.

Her face was devoid of color. Her nails had dug into the skin at her elbows until they were bloody. She was staring at the locks on the windows.

He had done this to her. By selfishly using the time they had to be physically close to her rather than prepare her for what was coming—this battle with Freihof—he'd tossed her back into this fight with no warning and no mental weapons.

"Natalie."

She didn't blink. He gently pried her hands from her arms. "Peaches."

She finally looked at him. Explaining to her again that they weren't going to let Freihof get to her wouldn't help. Instead, he drew her closer to the window.

"C'mon. I'll check the locks with you, okay?"

"I already know they're locked. But I can't stop checking. I know it's stupid, but I can't…"

He wrapped an arm around her and pulled her forward. "Sometimes we fight our demons. Sometimes we just learn to live with them. Either way, it's okay." They stepped forward and tried the lock of the first window together.

When they made it over to the second, he stopped her. "We'll finish checking all the locks, but before that, I want to give you something. Maybe it will help you feel better."

He pulled out the tiny piece of equipment Steve had given him. It was flat and not much larger than a dime, sticky on one side.

"This is a tracking device. Omega Sector agents often use something similar when they're on undercover missions. I'd like you to keep it on even when you get to Omega HQ tomorrow. That way I'll always be able to tell where you are."

"Will you be able to hear what I'm saying?"

He swallowed a smile at her natural inquisitive nature overtaking her fear for just a moment. "No, location only. It's not a communication device, so you can't hear me and vice versa."

"Where do I put it?"

He gently lifted her beautiful mane of blond hair from her shoulder and placed it behind her ear. "We've discovered this is the least obtrusive place for an agent to put it. If it becomes unsticky, just get it wet to reactivate the adhesive."

"Okay."

He reluctantly let her hair fall and moved his hand away from her neck with one more soft caress.

"And I have a phone for you, too." He handed her the little red device. "It doesn't have any bells or whistles, but you can use it to call me anytime once you get to Omega. Anytime. For any reason. It's going to be okay."

She tried to smile, but all the fear was back. "I know you believe that. I hope I'll be able to believe it soon, as well." She glanced back at the windows, tension once again strumming through her lithe body, and he knew her need to check them had returned.

"Let's finish double-checking the locks. Maybe then you can get some rest."

"I've already double-checked them," she whispered. "It will just get worse from here. I can't help it. I move from lock to lock, rechecking them even though I know I've already made certain they're secure."

He wanted to take her into his arms more than he wanted his next breath, but knew she would resist. Knew fighting him would just add to her burden.

"Can I help with anything?" Andrea stepped up next to them and asked.

"Do we have any sticky notes? Or even just paper and tape?" he asked her. "Natalie uses them to keep track of what locks she's checked."

Her face crumpled. "It's stupid, I know."

Andrea touched her on the arm. "Actually, it's a pretty smart coping mechanism that helps you keep situational OCD under control. Did a psychiatrist suggest it to you?"

"No, I came up with it on my own."

Andrea smiled. "Then I think it's even smarter. Let me see what I can find, then I'll help."

Ren turned around and found the rest of the team there.

"We'll all help," Steve said.

Natalie just stared at them. "B-but I'm your enemy," she finally stuttered.

"No, you're not." Ren kept his arm wrapped around her. "You've lost more than all of us at Damien's hands. And you're never going to fight him alone again. Now you've got a family who will fight with you."

"Let's get those locks checked," Steve said. "Because that's how family gets through things. Together."

NATALIE FINALLY FELL asleep on the couch with the lights on and everyone sitting and talking around her.

That was fine with Ren; he was going to have trouble letting her out of his sight until Freihof was caught. Even once she was at Omega HQ it wouldn't be easy for him.

Everyone had moved the conversation into the kitchen to give Natalie some quiet. Ren had stayed. Watching her from the chair next to the couch, wishing he had the right to scoop her up in his arms and hold her while she slept.

"I would say you've got it bad, brother, but I think you already know that." Steve, one of Ren's oldest friends and colleagues, took the chair across from him.

"That doesn't mean she's going to forgive me for what I did."

"Maybe. Maybe not. But at least at the end of the day, she'll be safe."

Ren nodded. If she couldn't forgive him, couldn't trust him again, he'd have to find a way to live with that. But Steve was right. At least he would know she was safe.

"I just got a call from Homeland."

Ren rolled his eyes. "Knew that was coming."

"We'll fight it. All of us. Everybody knows things happen in the field that are unexpected. You have to make decisions on the fly and sometimes—"

"I'm out, Steve." There wasn't any point in anyone taking a political bullet for him.

"Is that what you want?"

Ren shrugged again. "It's what I need. I've been under too long."

Steve studied him for a long minute. "Got other plans? Hell, Ren, you basically started Omega. It's been your baby all these years."

"Might be time to have a different kind of baby. I do believe you know a little something about that."

"Don't force me to get out pictures. My son is three months old now and I have at least one for every day of his existence." Steve chuckled before turning serious. "What will you do?"

"Go back to Montana, I think. I miss it. It wasn't until I was talking in such detail to Natalie about the farm that I realized how much."

Ashton stuck his head in from the kitchen. "You guys, we've got problems. This town isn't really equipped for the number of people we brought here with all the press, not to mention gawkers. There's a fight at the one bar in town and a fire has broken out at the hotel. Locals are asking for assistance."

Ren shot a look at Steve. "I'm not leaving Natalie."

"I'll send Brandon, Lillian and Ashton. This may be just what it seems like, too many people in a town with not enough amenities. But it doesn't change our overall mission. Freihof is the priority."

Ren looked over at Andrea, who wouldn't be going, and she just shrugged. "I'm not like Lillian in a fight—I'm more of a liability. And it would split Brandon's focus. He worries about me."

When the team left it was Ren's turn to pace from window to window—sidearm in hand. Dividing and conquering was definitely one of Freihof's MOs. Fire was, too.

But Ren would stand guard over Natalie while she slept. The magnitude of the fact that she trusted him enough, at least subconsciously, to sleep was not lost on him. Her brain had accepted that it was okay to shut down, that Ren wouldn't let anything happen to her.

And it was one hundred percent correct.

A couple hours later, looking a little worse for wear, the team returned. Yes, there had been fighting. Yes, also a fire. But nothing that suggested there was any further nefarious intent behind them.

Ren still didn't sleep. Even with the tracking device on her he wasn't sure he'd be able to sleep until he knew Natalie was safely within the fortitude of Omega HQ's walls. Nobody got in there.

He hated to wake her up a few hours later, knowing she needed the rest, and her body, which she'd abused so badly saving his life, needed to heal. But it was time. They were doing one last press conference before she was taken to Omega. After that, an agent of her general build and coloring would stay here for a few days to see if Freihof took the bait.

Ren didn't even want to think about what would happen if Freihof was more cautious than they gave him credit for. If he didn't come after Natalie—or who he thought was Natalie—over the next few days. If he decided to bide his time, wait for their guard to drop.

It would eat at Natalie's very sanity. And there wouldn't be a damned thing Ren could do about it except continuously put her in danger in hopes of luring Freihof out.

The entire team was exhausted but on high alert as they entered the school auditorium once again to meet the press. The county had given the kids the day off due to all the hoopla, but the school was packed with media and townspeople.

Ren kept his arm around Natalie as the mayor of Westwater introduced them. Ren stepped up to the podium, giving everyone his most charming smile. Their plan had to work this time. They needed to draw Freihof out.

"Thank you all for coming. As you can see, Natalie and I are alive and well." Out of the corner of his eye he saw her flinch at his use of her name. She was on to the fact that he said her name as much as possible. "We appreciate you even thinking we're newsworthy—"

"We don't!" someone screamed from the back of the room. "Get out of our town!"

Then Ren threw Natalie to the ground as shots rang out in the air and people began screaming.

Chapter Twenty-One

Natalie wasn't sure what was happening as Ren's weight rested on top of her, his hand keeping her head pinned protectively to the ground. She could vaguely hear panicked screams after a couple more shots were fired.

Ren kept them behind the large podium. A few minutes later Steve Drackett crawled over to them.

"Is it Damien?" she asked, trying to keep panic at bay.

"Not according to the sheriff." Steve kept low, like them. "Looks like it's some local troublemakers. Definitely heard shots fired from multiple locations, so that would make sense."

"We need to get you out of here. Back to the safe house," Ren said. "Then preferably immediately to Omega HQ. This little stunt—if it is, in fact, some local yokels—may change everything. May spook Freihof."

"It will definitely get a different type of media coverage now."

They crawled over to the side of the stage and then out the door. Ren and Steve kept her sandwiched between them, both of them with their guns in their hands, Ren with his arm wrapped firmly around her once they got off the stage, as they rushed to the side entrance.

A police car was waiting there in the small covered alley, as well as two police officers in their tan uniforms. Ren and Steve obviously already knew them both.

"Levell, Stutz, we need you to get Ren and Natalie back to the safe house and stay with them," Steve instructed the two younger men before turning to Ren. "I'm going to stay here. They'll need help with—"

A call came through loudly over Levell's police radio. "We've got a confirmed sighting of Freihof on the north side of the building. Exit that leads out to the playground!"

Natalie felt bile rising in her throat.

"That's Jensen," Stutz said. Both men looked ready to burst into action.

"No." Ren stopped them. "You two get her to the safe house. You don't leave her under any circumstances, you got it?"

He turned to Natalie. "We're going to catch him. Right now, okay? This is all going to be over soon." He threaded his hands into her hair and kissed her hard and fast. "And then I will find some way to make you forgive me and give us another chance."

Before she could say anything, he and Steve were gone. Sprinting in the direction of where Damien had been seen.

Desperate fear clawed up her belly. What if Damien killed Ren? She knew firsthand how diabolically brilliant her ex was.

"I can't believe we're this close to the action and have to be on babysitting detail instead," Levell said as he opened the squad car door for Natalie. "No offense."

"I think you're quite a bit closer to the action than you think."

Her whole world spun in a spiral of grayness as she heard the voice that haunted her nightmares. The one she hadn't heard in six years.

Damien.

She spun in time to see him raise a gun with a silencer on it and shoot first Levell, then Stutz, in the chest. Both men fell to the ground, not even able to draw their weapons. "Allow me to take over babysitting duty of my wife."

He turned to Natalie, smiling. "Hi, honey."

She opened her mouth to scream, but he brought the gun and placed it close to her cheek. "One sound and you'll be as dead as they are, wifey. Get in the car."

She stood rooted in place. If she went with Damien, she knew her life was over.

His eyes narrowed, the promise of violence clear in them. "If you don't get in the damn car right now, I will hunt down every single person in your beloved Omega Sector team and kill them slowly in front of you. You will do what I say, Natalie. You know what happens when you disobey."

She could feel the past coming back to crash over her, drowning her. His rules. His command. The knowledge that she had to be perfect like he wanted her to be or the pain would come.

She had to avoid the pain at all costs.

"Yes, sir." She got in the car; he followed, snatching her phone from her and keeping his gun trained on her.

"That's more like my perfect beauty."

They drove out of Westwater, Damien providing directions, Natalie following them. Once they were a few miles outside of town he had her pull over in a parking lot and change to a car he'd parked there. He put her in the passenger seat, zip-tying her wrists together, and got in behind the wheel.

She kept herself as far away from Damien as

she could, huddled over against the door. Trying to get her mind to work through the fear that seemed to swallow her whole.

"Looking at you last night, I thought all our training, our attempt to make you into the perfect wife we always knew you could be, had gone to waste." He reached over and stroked a finger down her arm. "But now I'm thinking maybe with some correction you can once again be trained to be perfect."

He hadn't touched her up to this point. The feel of his skin on hers tore something open in her.

"Do. Not. Touch. Me." She spat the words, dragging her arm away from his fingers.

He didn't even stop driving as he backhanded her. Natalie's face slammed into the window and she tasted blood.

"Evidently it will take a good deal more training to get you back to where you were. The perfect wife. I daresay I am up for the challenge."

"I was never your perfect wife. I left you. I ran away."

He shook his head. "You became confused. I'm willing to overlook that. You'll have to be punished for it, of course, but I am willing to give you another chance."

Something inside Natalie snapped further.

No. She would not go with him. Ren and the rest of the team would've figured out she was gone soon if not already. She had to slow Damien down.

"I pretended I was dead for six years rather than live one more minute with you, Damien. I wasn't confused."

That earned her another slap on her abused face. "You'd been shot by those careless bastards at Omega Sector. I saw all the blood. You couldn't have known what you were doing."

She reached up and wiped blood from her split lip. "Oh, but I did, Damien. I took the opportunity to run as far and as fast as I could from you. I knew exactly what I was doing when I made sure you would think I was dead and I hoped I would never see you again."

She saw his fists tighten on the steering wheel but she didn't care.

"I pretended to die to get away from you, Damien. I'd rather die for real than go back to being married to you. Omega Sector is going to find you and they're going to stop you."

Damien pulled over to the side of the back road and slammed on the brakes. He grabbed her hair and yanked her over until she was just inches from his face.

"Your precious Omega agents are going to have way too much on their hands to be worried about you. They're going to be busy dealing with the fallout from their own ineptitude."

"With your biological warfare canisters? Yeah, they know all about that."

He rolled his eyes. "I would hope so. If I'd made it any more obvious that it was me who had them, it would've had to be with engraved letterhead. But they don't know when and they don't know where, do they?"

He yanked her hair again, before letting go and starting the car once more. She reached up to touch her tender scalp and felt it. The tracker Ren had put at the back of her ear. She'd forgotten about it.

And Damien had no idea it was on her. All she needed to do was keep near him and it would lead the team right to them.

But Damien was never going to let them have her. She knew that. He would kill her before he would let her go, even if he was going to die, too. But at least they would stop him from whatever mad destruction he'd planned.

"The canisters are in the car even as we speak. I hadn't planned to use them all at one time in one location, but you helped me realize there's a blot in my past that needs to be erased. From now on, when I think of this place, it won't be because it was where you legally became mine, but because of what I did here today."

Natalie looked around more closely. "We're going back to Grand Junction?"

"Yes, to city hall, where we were married. To love and to honor. A vow you've decided to forget."

Just like he'd somehow forgotten *cherish and protect* when he'd broken all her fingers.

But as much as she wanted to stand up to Damien—and for the first time in her life she really did—she needed to lie. To remain docile. To distract him until Ren and his team could get here and stop him.

They drove in silence, Natalie struggling to figure out what to say, what to do, in order to stop Damien. Cry? Beg? He would love that. Could she do it? Maybe to save lives.

As they passed the city limits sign for Grand Junction, she knew she had to do *something*.

"Part of me missed you," she whispered, trying not to choke on the words.

"Is that so? Evidently not enough to return to me where you belong, even though you were my wife."

"You married someone else." Dissolving their marriage. Thank God.

"She looked like you. I thought she would be a better model, more easily trained. But when she decided to betray me, she had to be eliminated."

Natalie didn't even know how to respond to that. To the fact that he'd killed another woman who couldn't live up to his sick standards.

Damien drove in silence for many minutes.

"Tell me, Natalie. That man you were with out in the woods, the man you were hiking with, Warren Thompson. Were you intimate with him? Did you allow him to touch your body, which should've only ever belonged to me?"

"Damien…" Telling him the truth would only bring pain.

He shook his head as if overwhelmed by sadness. "You are not the person I'd hoped you'd be, Natalie."

"Can we go somewhere and talk? I don't want to go to city hall."

He looked over at her and smiled. "Yes, we can go somewhere. And I have no intention of taking you to city hall."

Good. That at least bought her—bought Ren—more time.

They drove to the other side of town and out of the most populated area. He turned into what looked like a field, driving through a gate, and down a paved road of some sort of park.

Then she realized what it was. A very high-end, private cemetery. "Damien, what is this place? Why are we here?"

"I want you to see your final resting place, my dear. The place where I buried an empty casket. The place I came to grieve my dead, perfect wife. I realize now that my wife did die six years ago. My wife would've never let another man touch her. I have no wife. And soon that casket won't be empty."

Natalie blanched as the truth hit her. There was no more time. He'd brought her here to kill her. She had to get away from him right now. Not even thinking about the consequence, Natalie reached over, yanked open the door and threw herself out of the car.

She cracked the ground with a bone-rattling thud and struggled through the pain to get up, her restrained hands hindering her. She heard Damien stop the car and forced herself to begin running toward the trees. As soon as she was off the road her feet became bogged down in snow.

She knew there wasn't any use. Damien was bigger. Stronger. Faster. But she pushed herself as fast as she could go. He still had her phone, so she'd have to pray the tracker would work.

And that she was buying Ren enough time to get to her.

She screamed as a hand grabbed her shoulder, jerking her down into the snow. The icy whiteness permeated everything.

"Thank you for at least running in the right direction," Damien said. He reached down and grabbed her by the hair, yanking her forward. She stumbled to keep up with him, since it was either that or be dragged.

"The minute you let someone touch your body you should've known you would never be worthy of me again. Now I'm grateful I had the foresight to buy such a private burial plot for you six years ago. Nobody ever comes out here."

He continued marching forward. She threw her hands up to his wrist to ease the pressure of the pull on her scalp. Finally, he stopped and threw her down and into the snow.

Right in front of a casket that had obviously just been dug out of the ground.

"Ironically, Omega Sector were the ones who dug it up. I guess it confirmed that you were alive. I can't believe you would choose them over me. I gave you a home. A life. Everything."

His foot came up and crashed against her midsection in a vicious kick. The shock hit her first—she couldn't inhale—and then the pain exploded. She curled herself in a ball, the cold seeping in everywhere.

"Remember how you used to beg me to let you out of the snow during your punishments, Natalie? I shouldn't have. I should've let you suffer and die out there. But now I'm going to let you suffer and die out *here*. You're going to be inside that casket, knowing that no one is ever coming for you."

"Damien, please…" She finally got words out. Her begging now wasn't to buy more time. It was in a desperate attempt to save her own life.

Could Ren possibly get here in time?

"I would love to stay here and watch you suffer, but I have a limited window of opportunity at city hall. I've got to give your Omega friends something to do with their time. A few thousand dead bodies ought to do it." He leaned down and whispered in her ear. "But don't worry, darling. I'll come by and visit your grave site often. Especially now that there will be a dead body to mourn."

Natalie closed her eyes, facing the facts. If Ren used the tracker to find her and she was already dead, they'd never be able to find Damien and stop him.

Thousands would die.

If she put the tracker on Damien now, the

team would go straight to him. Maybe they would be able to stop him.

But Natalie would die.

Silently, she wished she'd had the strength to tell Ren last night that she would've forgiven him. That she wished they'd had more time.

But now she would never have a chance.

She opened her eyes, reaching behind her ear and picking off the tracker. The wetness from her fingers immediately made it sticky again.

"One kiss?" she whispered to Damien.

She leaned in close and placed the tracker on the back of his neck as she touched him. She prayed it would be enough.

His lips touched hers and for once she was thankful the snow had numbed her and she couldn't feel a thing, especially his touch on her lips.

"The kiss of death," Damien said, smiling.

He picked her up and put her in the casket in the hole in the ground. She tried to keep her composure, her strength, her pride. Tried not to let Damien know the depths of her terror. But as the lid closed and she heard the thumping of earth being poured over her, she began to scream in terror.

She could hear Damien's laugh over it all.

Chapter Twenty-Two

Ren and Steve sprinted toward the north side of the school. Getting through the auditorium was nearly impossible with the pandemonium from the gunfire a few minutes ago. Chairs had been thrown everywhere. A few people had been hurt in their desperate need to evacuate.

They didn't stop. Unless someone was dying, they would have to wait for other assistance.

"Sheriff, tell your man not to engage Freihof," Steve was shouting into his walkie-talkie as he ran. "He is to be considered extremely dangerous whether he looks armed or not."

They burst through the door on the other side of the building, bringing them outside. Jensen, the deputy who'd called in the Freihof sighting, was waiting there, walkie-talkie in one hand, his phone in the other.

"Freihof ran off toward the trees." He looked

down at his phone again. "Hurry, maybe we can still catch him."

He and Steve bolted toward the trees, the deputy right behind them.

"Lillian—" Steve got on the walkie again "—Freihof's headed into the woods from the north side of the building."

Ren heard her curse. "Okay, Ashton and I are switching directions and heading straight into the woods from the east side. We'll try to cut him off."

"Do these woods lead anywhere? To a road? Another town?" Ren asked Jensen.

He shook his head. "Just more woods. It's all part of the McInnis Canyon National Park."

"He could be waiting to pick us off, Steve," Ren said as they slowed down, taking cover in the trees. Shooting from long range would be a little anticlimactic for Freihof, but Ren wouldn't put it past him.

"I can't figure out why he would even run in this direction at all." Steve said. "He's always used people for cover to get away, not nature."

Ren nodded. "Or why he wouldn't be in disguise. It's not like him to just rush into a situation where he can be easily identified."

They each kept a very careful eye for movement in the trees, progress frustratingly slow.

They didn't want to give Damien room to circle back around.

Eventually, they met up with Lillian and Ashton, who'd been coming from the opposite direction.

"Nothing?" Ren asked.

Lillian shook her head. "He didn't cross by us. He's either hiding or has gone farther out into the woods."

Brandon's voice came over the walkie-talkie. "I've got confirmation that it was definitely the Sheffield cousins, well-known troublemakers in this county, who were responsible for the shooting this morning. No one was hurt—they were just trying to create chaos because of, and I quote, 'All them peoples who think they can just piss on Westwater had another think coming.'"

Steve rolled his eyes. "Great."

"But I got hold of one of the Sheffields as he was being arrested and it ends up that it was someone matching Freihof's general description who gave them today's brilliant idea in the first place."

Ren stopped moving forward. "It was a brilliant idea to shake things up. To separate us. But not if he was just going to run into the damn wilderness. Only if he had a much bigger plan…"

Like separating him from Natalie.

He turned and looked at the deputy who'd led them this far. The man was sweating well beyond what should be normal for the slower speed they were moving and the man's overall fitness level.

"What did you do?" he asked, fear closing around his throat so tightly he could hardly breathe.

"I'm sorry." Jensen began to cry. "He sent me a picture of my wife and daughter, tied up. Said if I didn't tell you I'd seen him run into the woods he'd kill—"

Ren didn't wait to hear the rest; he turned and began running as fast as he could back toward the school.

"Levell, Stutz, come in," Steve yelled into the walkie-talkie. "Report. Sheriff, we need a report right damn now from Levell and Stutz. We left Natalie with them."

There was not a sound from them. Ren didn't even slow down to curse, just pushed his body faster than he ever had. He could hear Lillian and Ashton right behind him.

"I need any available officer to the south side of the auditorium," Steve was yelling into the walkie through panted breaths.

As Ren rounded the corner of the high school, someone stepped in front of him and he had to dodge to keep from knocking the guy over. He didn't so much as pause. Every fiber of his being was focused on getting back to Natalie.

He ripped open the door on the far side of the auditorium, leaping over fallen chairs and broken camera stands, bolting up to the stage and out the back door where he'd taken Natalie not thirty minutes before.

Weapon still in hand, he burst through the outer door that led to the alley.

His worst nightmare met him there: two fallen officers lying in puddles of blood and Natalie nowhere in sight.

He planted himself on the ground beside Levell to check for a pulse while someone else did the same on Stutz.

Ren shook his head. There was nothing. Levell was dead. Kid hadn't been wearing his vest.

"I've got a pulse here," Lillian said, reaching in to put pressure on the wound. "But tell the ambulance to hurry the hell up."

Ren stood and looked at Steve. "I gave Natalie the tracker last night. We can follow her, but I've got to get to the safe house to get the computer with the program."

Steve nodded, still talking to emergency services. Lillian stayed with Stutz, but Ashton took off running with Ren. They were in the house, booting up the laptop, when Ashton spoke.

"If Freihof was talking to those jerks last night, inciting them to riot this morning, then he either got exceptionally lucky or he already knew about this little plan."

He'd known. The bastard had known they were coming to Westwater before they'd even gotten there. "I think he has some sort of tap on Steve's Omega phone. It's the only means I've used to communicate anything about Natalie. Freihof is the one who tortured and killed the owners of the Santa Barbara beach house, probably to try to get answers for what info was missing from the phone calls. But he definitely knew Natalie and I would get here last night. Steve and I talked about that specifically."

"You think the fire and fight last night were instigated by him, too?"

Why the hell was the computer taking so damn long to boot? "Undoubtedly."

"We're going to get her back," Ashton whispered as they both stared at the screen.

Had someone told him this when Freihof had taken Ashton's wife, Summer, and her daughter, Chloe? Ren hoped it had worked better than the words of comfort were working on him right now.

He knew what Freihof was capable of. Knew the ways he had tortured Natalie.

Knew she had to be scared out of her mind right now. Freihof had nearly forty-five minutes on them.

The ways someone could hurt another person in forty-five minutes had Ren breaking out in a cold sweat.

The computer finally booted and Ren started the program that would track Natalie, breathing a sigh of relief when he saw the dot on the map was still moving. Movement meant life.

He connected the 4G from his phone to the laptop. "Let's roll. We'll be able to get a more accurate location as we get closer."

Ashton jogged with him to the car. "Where are we headed?"

"Grand Junction."

"Anything special about that place?"

"Definitely to Freihof."

REN CURSED UNDER his breath when the tracker stopped. Ashton was already driving well over one hundred miles per hour. The rest of the team—Steve, Lillian, Brandon—were five minutes behind them. A number of other Omega Critical Response team members were on their way to Grand Junction via helicopter.

Damien Freihof was going down today. He

would never hurt anyone else again; these agents were going to make sure of it.

Ren just prayed it was in time to save Natalie. That she—who had suffered the most at Freihof's hands already—would not be his last victim.

Before they could home in on an exact location, the tracker began moving again. A few minutes later it stopped again. And stayed stopped this time. When Ren realized where it was he cursed out loud.

"What?" Ashton said.

"They're at city hall."

"Why would he go there?"

Ren grimaced. "That's where he and Natalie got married nearly ten years ago." He called Steve and put it on speakerphone.

"The tracker stopped at city hall. I think Freihof is trying to make some sort of sick romantic gesture, marry Natalie again."

Over Ren's dead body.

"How far out are you?" Steve asked.

"Maybe six minutes," Ashton responded, never letting up on the speed.

"Okay, we're right behind you. Everybody get your comm units on, channel one."

"Steve." Ren couldn't hide the desperation in his voice. "He's not going to let her go willingly. If we go barreling in there, we might get Freihof, but we'll lose Natalie."

"That's not going to happen. Neither the barreling nor the losing Natalie. Ashton, city hall probably isn't going to have a lot of windows, but see if you can find a vantage point on a neighboring roof once we know what room they're in, in case it comes down to a long-distance shot."

"Roger that, boss."

"We'll get Lillian up in an air duct," Steve continued. "Nobody ever expects the ass-kicking midget dropping out of the ceiling."

In the background, Ren could hear Lillian's choice words at that description.

"We've got Roman and Derek coming with heavier firearms and expertise on explosives. And even Joe Matarazzo, just in case negotiations will help."

In other words, the entire Omega team.

A few minutes later, they were pulling up in front of city hall. Steve was still giving out orders as to who would handle what, since a priority would be clearing the building as much as possible before anything went down.

This was Steve's team. Ren may have been the one who originally created Omega Sector, but Steve had turned the Critical Response Division into a well-oiled machine.

"She's in an office in the southwest corner of the building," Ren said, reading the information from the tracker into the comm unit.

"According to building plans," Derek spoke from the helicopter, "that's the wedding licensing section."

Ashton grabbed his sharpshooter rifle and sprinted toward the roof of the building next door.

Ren waited for the rest to arrive, ushering civilians out and away from the outside of the building. It went against his every instinct not to burst in on his own. But Steve was right; if there was anything that Freihof had taught Omega Sector in his attacks over the past few months it was that their greatest strengths were in how they worked together.

Within a few minutes the rest of the team was there, moving into position with a silent nod at Ren. Immediately, they began to get as many people out of the building as possible. Local police were showing up to help, setting up barricades. Seeing the team, how capable and functional they all were, Ren had his first sense of true hope.

Until Ashton spoke into the comm unit from his spot on the roof.

"Uh, guys, I've got eyes on Freihof and we've got some bad news. He has a pressure switch in his hand. If I take a shot, whatever he's rigged to explode is going with him. And given that he has multiple canisters of that biological contaminant, I'm going to assume that's what he has planned to go."

Ren cursed under his breath. "Is Natalie okay?"

"Natalie's not with him at all."

Chapter Twenty-Three

"Are you sure she's not with him?" Ren asked.

"At least she's not in that room," Ashton responded. "It's got big windows with no curtains, so I've got a pretty unobstructed view."

"I can confirm," Lillian chimed in from her location. "Damn it, I can't get all the way over to that set of offices from this air duct, but I can see them from this vent. Freihof is just standing here, like he's reminiscing. And no Natalie. But, Ren, I think in Freihof's other hand is Natalie's red phone."

Ren cursed under his breath. How the hell was the tracker in the room if Natalie wasn't? If she wasn't there, where the hell was she?

"Lillian, do you think he's about to blow the whole building?" Steve asked.

"I don't know. But we need to do something fast. Because clearing the building if he uses that biological weapon is not going to help. It will spread. Radius will be devastating."

Ren turned to Steve. "I'm calling him on Natalie's phone. If he's about to release that pressure trigger, we need to do something to distract him. He doesn't know we're here, and I won't let him know. Let's just get as many people out and back as far as possible without causing a panic."

Steve nodded, and the rest of the team immediately began moving fast around him.

"I'll keep trying to find a way to get closer so I can get the drop on him," Lillian said. "It might mean crawling back to the other side of the building and coming in from that direction."

Ashton added, "Ren, I need a word or phrase that lets me know to take him out. I don't think a direct shot is a good option with the pressure trigger, but we need one, anyway. I'll aim for the chest."

"Let's go with 'reign of terror.'"

"Appropriate. Roger that."

"Get him mad," Brandon came on the line and said. "He won't take himself—and hopefully everyone else—out if he's angry at you. Make him mad enough that he wants to live to come after you."

Ren pulled out his phone and dialed the number for the one he'd given to Natalie.

"Who's this?" he asked when Freihof answered, like he didn't already know.

"Who's this?" Freihof responded in kind.

"Let me talk to Natalie."

"I'm sorry. I'm afraid Natalie isn't here right now."

"And this is?" Ren wasn't sure exactly how to play this most effectively. Did Freihof know about Ren? That he was part of Omega?

"I'm Natalie's husband, Damien. You must be her…friend, Warren."

"I think you mean ex-husband, right, Damien? Since you remarried and all?"

"I never would've remarried if I had known my Natalie was alive. So as far as I'm concerned, that means we're still married."

Ren sighed dramatically and walked inside city hall. He didn't want Freihof to hear any activities or sirens and become suspicious. "Well, as far as the law—and every logical person on the planet—is concerned, when you signed a divorce decree from her, you officially became unmarried. No matter what you want."

There was a long moment of silence. "And why does it matter to you, Warren?"

"Because she's mine now, Damien. She's done with you and she's chosen me. That's just the way it is."

"No, that's not how it is at all." The words were bit out. "Not at all."

"Why don't you just let me talk to her, okay? Or maybe the three of us can meet somewhere and figure out the answer to this. Nobody has to get hurt. Just put Natalie on the phone, okay?"

"No, the choices have already been made. Natalie knew if she didn't choose me, then she wouldn't be choosing anyone."

Ice formed in Ren's veins. Was he too late? Was Natalie already dead? Or stuffed in a closet somewhere here, hurt? He hit the mute button on the phone and spoke into the comm unit.

"Steve, make sure your people are checking the utility closets and small spaces where he might have put Natalie."

"Roger that."

Ren unclicked the mute button. "Tell me where she is, Freihof."

Natalie had put the tracker on Freihof, so that gave Ren a measure of hope. She had to have been alive when she did that. But it could've been moments before her death, realizing Damien would leave once she was gone, and Omega would have no way of knowing where. That they would come to her rather than follow him.

And it was true. If Ren knew where Natalie was right now, he would leave this situation—damn the consequences—and find her. He refused to believe she was dead.

Freihof just laughed. "You know, I came to this place because it held special memories for me. Memories of a time before my relationship with Natalie became so tainted. She was so innocent when we first got married, do you know that? I thought she could become the perfect wife. I tried to teach her that."

"By abusing her?"

"Now, Warren." Freihof tsked. "You weren't there. You don't know. Some people might think my methods were a little harsh. But they were necessary. I was trying to make her *perfect*. Isn't that what everyone ultimately wants? Natalie would've thanked me eventually."

"Instead, she pretended she was dead and ran away and hid. Doesn't sound like thanking to me."

Freihof sighed. "I was feeling sad when I got here. Feeling that now that I was never going to see Natalie again, maybe it was time for me to die, too. That I would also just go out in the chaos I create."

Ren felt like all the oxygen had been sucked from the room. "Freihof…"

"But the good news is, talking to you has

made me realize that it's not my time yet. That I want to see the fallout of my actions and how they affect Omega Sector. After all, they are the ones who took Natalie from me in the first place. She may have chosen to stay away from me—a sin she is currently regretting, at least for a little while longer—but Omega is what gave her the opportunity to run. You've made me realize I need to stay my course. It is not my destiny to die here today."

"Where is she, Freihof? If she's not with you, tell me where she is."

"No, Warren Thompson, you tell me *who* you are. I could find no record of you at all inside Omega Sector. No pictures in the files. You're so unimportant that you don't have a significant file yet. So, honestly, I'm not sure you're worth my time to talk to."

Ashton's voice came in Ren's ear. "Freihof's getting agitated. If he moves out of this office I might lose the shot."

"She chose me, Freihof. This whole plan in the woods may have started just with the intent to catch you, but we fell for each other. She chose me. Natalie is mine."

"No!" The word came through so loud Ren had to hold the phone away from his ear. "Natalie is *mine*."

"No, she's not, Damien. And you've always

known that, haven't you? Tried to make her into something fake. Called it 'perfect' so you could justify abusing her. She chose me, you bastard."

The phone line clicked dead in his hand.

"Okay, it's working." It was Ashton's voice again. "He's taking off his explosives vest and placing it on... Oh, hell, there are the canisters. The biological contaminant canisters are definitely in the room with him. It looks like he's setting some sort of timer, but he's still got the kill switch in his hand."

Ren had to make his move now. "Steve, I'm going in. I've got to stop him. If he gets out we'll lose our shot and he'll blow the canisters, anyway. Ashton, be ready."

"We've gotten most of the civilians clear and locals are getting them back to the safety point. Every hazmat team in the state is on their way here," Steve said.

"Did anyone find Natalie in the building?"

"No, brother. I'm sorry."

"Okay, get your team out. Once I'm close enough to grab the pressure trigger and give Ashton the signal, he'll take him out. But we don't need to risk more lives."

"I'm staying," Lillian piped in.

"Me, too." That was Derek Waterman, SWAT leader.

One by one, the rest of the Critical Response unit chimed in. None of them would be leaving. They'd lost too much at Freihof's hands.

"I think you've got your answer, Ren. We take this bastard down together."

Ren dialed the number again as he walked down the corridor of city hall toward the office where Freihof was located.

"Warren," Freihof said as he answered. "I'm busy. I don't have time to talk to you anymore."

"I think you do, Freihof. Especially since I haven't quite been honest with you."

"Oh, yeah, about what?"

Ren opened the door to the office and ended the call. Freihof spun around, eyes wide.

"The fact that I'm here in city hall, for one thing," Ren said.

Freihof immediately held out the pressure trigger in front of him. "Stay back. If I let go of this trigger, this entire building is going to blow. So if you decide to shoot me, we die together."

Ren took out his sidearm and laid it on the ground, then did the same with his ankle holster. "I'm not going to shoot you." He kicked them both away.

"How did you know where I was?"

He needed to convince Freihof that he really was just a peon in Omega and he was here alone. "I figured it out when you said that you were somewhere that was special to you and Natalie. I know you got married here."

"And all your Omega buddies?"

Ren took a tiny step forward. "You're right. Nobody is very interested in hearing what a peon has to say. They're all out searching your previous property and places you were known to go. I told them I was coming here but none of them would listen."

Freihof scoffed and relaxed just slightly. Ren took the opportunity to take another step toward the man.

"That's the problem with Omega. They're so gung-ho for action. Always with the working harder rather than smarter. Don't truly think like a *team*."

"Oh, I think they can when it's truly important. I just don't think I'm part of the team." Another half step. He was about eight feet from Freihof now. "Where is Natalie? That's all I care about."

"I'm afraid my wife will no longer be available to play the whore for you, Mr. Thompson."

"Is she dead?"

Freihof looked down at the phone in his hand and Ren quickly took another step forward.

"She's not dead yet. Although right about now I'd say she's probably wishing she was."

Ren swallowed the fear and fury Freihof's words ignited. "Tell me where she is and I'll let you go."

The other man laughed heartily. "See, this is the problem with newbies. You think you have control of the situation, but you don't. You don't get to tell me when I go or don't go, because I'm the one holding the pressure trigger." Freihof put the phone down on a chair next to a wall and picked up one of the guns Ren had kicked away. "And now I'm holding your gun. So I'm afraid I'm going to walk out of here right after I shoot you."

"Ren?" Ashton's voice was in his ear. "I've still got the shot."

Ren gave a slight shake of his head.

"Ren says no." This time it was Lillian's voice in his ear. Ashton would only have his sights trained on Freihof, and wouldn't be able to see Ren.

It wasn't time yet. Now that Freihof had weapons, he was feeling more secure. Ren was able to take another step closer under the guise of dejection. He was almost close enough. Would almost be able to take the leap and catch the pressure trigger once Ashton took his shot.

"Holding until the go phrase is given," Ashton muttered. "But hurry up or he's going to shoot you, Ren."

"My name isn't Warren Thompson." Another step.

Freihof's eyes narrowed. "So? I don't really care what your name is. Soon you'll be dead."

"My name is Ren McClement."

"I've still never heard of you."

Ren shook his head. "No, you wouldn't have. I'm not part of the Critical Response unit. I'm not part of any official Omega unit. Look at me, Freihof. Do I look like I'm a newbie?"

There. The last step he needed. Freihof actually took it for him.

For the first time Freihof didn't look totally in control. "Wh-what?"

"You're trying to finish Omega Sector? Then it's probably fitting that you meet me as you go down. I *created* Omega Sector, and it will not be destroyed by the likes of you. Your reign of terror is over."

Ren didn't wait to see if Ashton would shoot at the agreed upon words, just knew he would. Ren dove toward Freihof's arm that held the detonator, his hands closing over it as the force of Ashton's bullet ripped through Freihof's torso. They both ended up lying on the ground.

Blood was pouring out of Freihof's chest but he still brought the gun in his other hand up and pointed it at Ren, smiling. Ren couldn't let go of the trigger device to save himself.

But then another bullet hit Freihof's hand and knocked the gun out of it, at the same time yet another bullet came from a different direction. Freihof screamed, his arm falling to the side, useless.

Lillian lowered herself from the air-conditioning vent. "Nobody ever expects the ass-kicking midget dropping out of the ceiling."

"Or the really pissed-off SWAT member waiting outside the door," Roman Weber, whose shot had hit Freihof's shoulder, said. "I was in a coma for over a week because of you, you bastard, and you sent my pregnant woman to what would've been sure death."

The blood flowing from Freihof's wounds left him with just a few more seconds left to live. The rest of the Omega team filed in, but Ren ignored them.

"Where is she, Damien? This is over. Tell me where Natalie is."

Ren could hear the pleading in his voice, but he didn't care. He would beg, threaten, grovel…whatever would get him Natalie back.

"My perfect wife. She wouldn't have wanted to live without me." His breaths wheezed in and out of his chest as more blood pooled on the floor. "I had nobody to bury last time. But this time I did. You may have saved your precious Omega, but you won't save—"

Freihof's eyes closed and his body went slack.

"No!" Ren screamed the word. Steve's hands closed over his and took the pressure trigger from him as Ren grabbed Freihof by his shirt. "Tell me where she is, damn it! Tell me."

But Freihof would never be telling anyone anything ever again.

And Natalie, his first victim, would also be his last.

As the team began preparing the canisters for containment, Steve put his hand on Ren's shoulder.

"She could be anywhere," Ren whispered. "If she's still alive at all. He could've buried her in the snow, like he used to do to torture her."

Although this time there wouldn't be anyone to let her out when she begged for mercy.

"She could be at his house. The house they lived at."

Steve nodded. "We're sending locals over there right now. They'll search every inch of that property."

Brandon Han burst through the door. "Andrea figured it out. It's Freihof's last words about not having a body to bury the first time, but now he did. We had the grave site exhumed two weeks ago when we found out Natalie was alive."

"Where?"

Brandon gave the address.

Ren didn't even respond, just sprinted out of the hallway and to his car. He knew beyond a shadow of a doubt that Brandon and Andrea were correct.

Damien had buried Natalie in her own coffin.

Chapter Twenty-Four

At some point Natalie's screams died off to raspy whispers. She had no idea how long she'd been inside the casket—minutes? Hours? Eternity?

She'd tried to have the presence of mind enough to push at the lid. To attempt to bring her legs up so she could use them as leverage to push. But no matter what she did, it wouldn't budge.

She tried not to think of all the dirt and snow piled on top of her. Because now when she screamed with her broken voice it was just silent, which was somehow worse.

She had lived silent and alone and broken for so many years and now she was going to die silent and alone and broken.

She faded in and out; the moments of nothing were pure bliss that ended too soon. When she would come to, she would have a moment of trying to fight the panic before it would overwhelm her. She ripped at everything. Her clothes. Her hair. The skin of her neck. She knew when her fingers came away wet she had drawn her own blood.

She wished so badly she had kept the tracker on her own body rather than put it on Damien. She didn't care how selfish it was. Then Ren would've found her. Would've gotten her out of here.

Finally, everything began to fade to a distance. She felt like she was floating. Almost swaying. Maybe she was running out of oxygen. How long could one survive buried underground?

Through the fog she swore she could almost hear somebody calling her name, but knew that couldn't be right. Her brain had finally broken completely and was playing tricks on her. The movement she felt had to be her own shudders. Surely this had to be near the end.

"Natalie, can you hear me?"

Yes, Ren, I can hear you. She didn't try to say the words since her voice was so wrecked. Plus, he wasn't really here, anyway.

"Hang on, Peaches, I'm coming."

The noises got louder. The jolting more pronounced. And then Natalie saw something she thought she was never going to see again.

Sunshine. She had to blink against the brightness of it.

"Oh, my God." Ren's hands were in her hair, over her heart, running up and down her arms. His lips were all over her face, her cheeks, her eyes, her hair. When he drew back his hands he stared at her blood.

He sat back up and yelled over his shoulder. "She's here. She's hurt. Get an ambulance."

His deep, strong voice broke on the last word. She wanted to tell him that she was okay. That she'd done that to herself in her panic.

"Ren…" Her voice came out in a whisper. She couldn't say anything else even if she wanted to. She slipped her arms around his neck as he lifted her out of the place she'd known she would die.

He stayed next to her as the paramedics placed her in the ambulance, answering questions she wasn't able to answer. Stayed with her as the doctors checked her at the hospital, explained about the damage to her vocal cords that would eventually heal and bandaged the superficial damage she'd done to her neck with her own fingernails.

Ren explained that Damien was dead. And the next day, as morbid as it sounded, he'd wheeled her down to the morgue so she could see the body for herself. And know there was no chance Damien was ever coming back.

Ren stayed by her side the first night in the hospital, holding her hand as he slept in a reclining chair beside her.

And through it all she hadn't said a word to him.

She couldn't talk to Ren. And not just because of the damage to her voice.

She couldn't talk to him because she needed space. Needed to find herself. Needed to know what her life was on her own without the constant companionship of fear and panic.

It had nothing to do with not trusting Ren and everything to do with figuring out a way to trust herself.

When Ren went out to talk to Steve and some of the other Omega people the second day, Andrea slipped in to say hello.

"How are you?" she asked. "I know you can't really talk. But I just wanted to say that I'm glad you're okay. I don't know how much anyone told you, but basically Omega has been under siege by Freihof for months. In my case, longer. So we're all glad he's gone and we're truly thankful for the role you played in taking him down. Putting that tracker on him under those circumstances was an exceptionally brave thing to do."

Natalie just shrugged, given how she'd cursed herself for that decision.

"Is there anything I can do for you?" Andrea asked. She stepped in closer. "Natalie, I'm not just talking get-you-a-soda type stuff, although I'll certainly do that. I know what it's like to feel like you have nothing. To need a chance to find yourself before you can do anything else."

Natalie took the pad of paper next to her bed that she'd been using to communicate.

I'm not trying to hurt Ren. I'm not angry. But I just can't be with him right now.

Andrea smiled, understanding and sadness tinting her eyes. "You need to heal. Nobody would begrudge you that. Least of all Ren."

Andrea sat down next to her, and together they worked out a plan.

Six months later

NATALIE SAT ON the deck of another beach house in Santa Barbara. This one was quite a bit smaller than the one where she'd house-sat months ago. And a couple of blocks from the beach itself. Andrea and the Omega Sector team had helped her find it and, using money confiscated from accounts linked to Damien, had bought it outright for her.

Combat pay, they'd called it.

The house had become her saving grace.

It was here that she'd cried her eyes out for the teenager she'd been who'd made such a bad decision in who she'd married and paid such a steep price for it in the years to come. Here that she'd ranted and slammed dishes on the ground when she thought of the six more years of her life that she'd lost by running and hiding and living in terror.

At first she couldn't even look at a pack of sticky notes without feeling shame. But then Andrea, who had become a regular visitor, had pointed out—for both of their cases—that someone never needed to apologize for the way they had chosen to survive. And more importantly, that Natalie didn't need the sticky notes any longer. That was the most important thing.

Other members of Omega Sector had come by to visit also those first few weeks, some Natalie had seen before, others she hadn't.

Roman Weber, a member of the SWAT team, brought his very pregnant soon-to-be-wife, Keira, also a good friend of Andrea's. They explained how Freihof had nearly killed them both—on two separate occasions—and thanked her for what she'd done to help stop him.

Tiny, tough SWAT member and occasional bus-ticket-saleswoman Lillian brought her man, Jace, by. They told her the story of how Damien had almost blown up a huge chunk of Denver, and brought Lillian's worst nightmare back into her life. They thanked Natalie for making sure they would never have to worry about Damien again.

And sharpshooter Ashton, whom Natalie had found out was the one to put the bullet into Damien, brought his new wife and adopted toddler daughter, Chloe, by. She'd played with the adorable little girl for hours on the beach and then set up a little easel for her to paint when she'd expressed interest in Natalie's own pictures.

"Because of your strength and courage, the world is a better place," Ashton had said in her ear the next day as he'd hugged her goodbye. "You're part of the Omega family now. You and Ren both, even though he's not working there anymore."

"He's not?" She couldn't stop herself from asking, the same way she hadn't been able to stop herself from thinking about him or dreaming about him.

"Nope. Went back to work on some sheep farm in Montana. Go figure. Said it was where half his heart was. And that he was hoping the other half would get there soon."

Steve Drackett showed up the next day, a small dog kennel in one hand. He did not look amused.

"I've known Ren McClement for more than fifteen years. He's saved my life more than once. Please tell him when you see him that, after this little stunt, I consider my debt to him well and truly paid."

He set the crate on the ground and opened it. A puppy came bounding out.

A damned Old English sheepdog puppy.

A *sheepdog*.

Steve handed her a card.

This little guy might look out of place in Santa Barbara. But he'd be perfect in Montana.

Natalie grabbed the tiny ball of white fur and pulled him up into her arms, giggling as he licked her face over and over.

"Aren't you just the most adorable thing I've ever seen? I shall call you… Cream."

Steve had just rolled his eyes. "Damn thing howled the entire way here. Tell Ren that next time he has to do his own dirty work."

But Steve had winked at Natalie, so she knew he wasn't truly mad.

Cream became her constant companion, his unconditional affection helping to heal Natalie in ways she hadn't even known she had been broken. She wanted to write Ren, call him, something. But couldn't quite make herself do it.

The next month the first postcard arrived. It was obviously over ten years old and had a picture of sunny Barcelona, Spain, on the front.

I realized I'd never sent these while I was in the army because I never had someone I wanted to share my life with. You are that person. Yours, Ren.

A couple days later another old postcard, this one from Istanbul, Turkey, showed up.

Growing up, I loved to read but my friends teased me about it, so I used to hide it, only reading while I lay under the covers at night. Yours, Ren.

Every few days, another postcard from his collection would arrive. And on the back, some small truth about his life that would help her to know him better. Some funny. Some heart-breaking. But always honest.

Day sixty-two. Tallinn, Estonia.

I want to give you new memories of the snow. To teach you how to make snow angels. Yours, Ren.

Tears leaked out of her eyes as she read this one, and then them all, over and over again. How could she explain to him that she had long since made peace with the fact that he'd just been doing his job when he'd tricked her. That after talking with the people from Omega—and having experienced Damien's horrific violence herself—that she understood that Damien had to be stopped no matter what.

She was just afraid she was too broken to ever be the woman Ren deserved to have.

Day one hundred and five. Bari, Italy.

We don't have to have all the answers now. We will figure them out as we go. Yours, Ren.

She painted. Day in and day out. Scenes of the ocean. Of Cream. Of people. Of storms she witnessed. But mostly of that beautiful spot in the wilderness looking down on the river.

When she finally got enough guts to show them to a gallery they surprised her by immediately wanting to put on a private show of just her work.

The show came and went the next month and Natalie was flabbergasted by the fact that nearly every single piece had sold and at quite a hefty price.

She was going to be able to make it on her own.

And that was when she realized she didn't want to. She wanted to be beside Ren—to share every part of her life with him. She could paint anywhere. And where she really wanted to paint the most was at a farm in Montana that she'd never seen.

It was time.

The next day she sent *him* a postcard.

Santa Barbara. Montana. Any of the places on your postcards. As long as it's you and me together. Yours, Peaches.

When a knock came on the door that night, she opened it, never expecting it could be Ren. But it was.

"What— How— I just sent the postcard this morning!"

His fingers were in her hair, pulling her close. She breathed in his scent, arms slipping around him.

"I ran out of patience—and postcards—last week. I was here to beg, grovel, do whatever I needed to do to get you back into my life. We can take it slow, or we can drive to Vegas tonight and get married. But please, Peaches, just tell me you will be with me."

She smiled. "Yes. Like you said, we'll work out the details as we go. But…yes."

His arms wrapped around her hips, pulling her up to him so he could kiss her. Gently. Reverently. Kisses that stole her breath. Stole her heart.

"As much as I'd like to stay here doing this for the rest of the night—hell, the rest of my *life*—there's something nibbling on my ankle."

Natalie giggled. "That would be Cream. I think you're to blame for him."

A smile full of reverence softened his face. "I'll take the blame for anything that causes you to make that sound and your face to light up like that. I plan to take every bad memory you have and replace each one with a dozen new good ones."

He set Natalie down so she could pick up Cream.

"That might take a long time."

He kissed her. "That's okay, Peaches." Then smiled at the pup who was busy licking both their faces. "And Cream. We've got forever."

* * * * *

Look for more books from USA TODAY *bestselling author Janie Crouch in 2019!*

Get 4 FREE REWARDS!

We'll send you 2 FREE Books plus 2 FREE Mystery Gifts.

Harlequin® Romantic Suspense books feature heart-racing sensuality and the promise of a sweeping romance set against the backdrop of suspense.

FREE
Value Over
$20

Get 4 FREE REWARDS!

We'll send you 2 FREE Books
<u>plus</u> 2 FREE Mystery Gifts.

Harlequin Presents* books feature a sensational and sophisticated world of international romance where sinfully tempting heroes ignite passion.

FREE
Value Over
$20